FLIGHT OF THE OUTCASTS

ZONDERVAN

Flight of the Outcasts
Copyright © 2010 by Alister McGrath
Illustrations © 2010 by Wojciech Voytek Nowakowski

This title is also available as a Zondervan ebook.
Visit www.zondervan.com/ebooks.

Requests for information should be addressed to:

Zondervan, *Grand Rapids, Michigan* 49530

This edition: ISBN 978-0-310-72193-2 (softcover)

Library of Congress Cataloging-in-Publication Data

McGrath, Alister E., 1953-
    Flight of the outcasts / by Alister E. McGrath.
       p. cm.–(The Aedyn chronicles ; bk. 2)
    Summary: Trying to run away from their horrid stepmother and her children, Peter
and Julia find themselves back in the mysterious land of Aedyn with their stepsister
Louisa along, where they discover that the people of Aedyn are being held captive and
forced to work on a distant island at the foot of an active volcano.
    ISBN 978-0-310-71813-0 (hardback)
    [1. Fantasy. 2. Brothers and sisters—Fiction. 3. Good and evil—Fiction. 4.
Volcanoes—Fiction.] I. Title.
PZ7.M169477Fl 2011
[Fic]–dc22   2010045041

Published in association with the literary agency of Alive Communications, Inc., 7680 God-
dard Street, Suite 200, Colorado Springs, CO 80920, www.alivecommunications.com.

Zonderkidz is a trademark of Zondervan.

Editor: Kathleen Kerr
Art direction: Cindy Davis
Cover design: Sarah Molegraaf
*Interior design and composition: Luke Daab, Carlos Eluterio Estrada, Greg Johnson/Text-
book Perfect*

Printed in the United States

11 12 13 14 15 16 /DCI/ 23 22 21 20 19 18 17 16 15 14 13 12 11 10 9 8 7 6 5 4 3 2 1

THE AEDYN CHRONICLES

BOOK TWO

FLIGHT OF THE OUTCASTS

Alister McGrath

ZONDERVAN.com/
AUTHORTRACKER
follow your favorite authors

CHAPTER

1

The December wind whipped against the cliffs of the English Channel and surged north, rattling windowpanes and beating against doorways as it went. It howled over the moors and valleys until finally it came knocking at the window of the Queen's Academy for Young Ladies.

And with the wind came rain. It started slowly: first just a few drops streaking against the glass, then more, and then, all of a sudden, a downpour washing over the view. The branches of the willow bent and scraped against the window, and Julia Grant, sitting at her desk with chin in hand, thought it must be the loneliest sound in the world.

It was an opinion that was certainly shared by her classmates. Every girl in the room was staring out the window and dreaming of the Christmas holidays, of three whole weeks of parties and cakes and presents. So perhaps Miss Wimpole, who was trying valiantly to fill her students' heads with a lesson on Sir Francis Drake and the defeat of the Spanish Armada, could be forgiven for snapping so harshly as she called them back to attention.

Julia's head snapped up at the sound of Miss Wimpole's voice. She scribbled a few notes from the blackboard into her workbook, writing in her neat, tiny handwriting, but after only a moment she was back to gazing out the window, watching the twigs making little tracks in the water as the wind pushed them to and fro. She—perhaps alone among all her classmates—was not looking forward to the Christmas holidays. Christmas meant home, and home meant horrid Bertram and horrider Louisa, and worst of all her new stepmother.

Julia's mother had died two years before, and Julia and her brother, Peter, had come to expect that their holidays would be spent with their grandparents in Oxford when their father, Captain Grant, was away at sea. But after one such holiday the previous spring he had arrived home unexpectedly and announced his engagement to a widow with two children. They had been married before the month was out.

His new wife was a tall, angular woman with a tight smile and cold grey eyes. Her children, Bertram and Louisa, were spoiled and mean and liked to torment their pet cat for sport. Peter thought that probably they were all criminals on the run from the law. His ears had been boxed for saying so in front of their father.

"All right, class. That will be all for today," Miss Wimpole was saying. Julia came to attention once again, realizing that her notes trailed off during a particularly dry section on the English ships' cast-iron cannons and never picked back up. She hoped England had won. "Have a marvelous holiday." Miss Wimpole stood at the blackboard with a strangled smile on her face as a flurry of activity erupted around her: chairs and desks scraping across the floor, papers rustling, books slamming shut, and twenty eager girls fleeing the room. Julia, sitting at the back of the classroom, was last in line, and Miss Wimpole touched the sleeve of her dress before she could leave.

"Stay and chat a bit, will you?" she asked, and Julia nodded. She clutched her books and papers against her chest while Miss Wimpole sat down on the edge of her big desk.

"I'm a bit worried about you, Julia," she said gently. "You seem so distracted since last term. Your thoughts are far away, and your grades—well, we don't have to talk about your grades, do we?"

Julia shook her head.

Miss Wimpole cleared her throat. "I just wanted to see if everything at home is … is as it should be. It can't have been easy—losing your mother and having the Captain remarry so quickly …" Her voice trailed off, and Julia realized that she was meant to respond.

"I'm fine," she said. "Everything's fine."

"Ah," said Miss Wimpole. "I suppose, then …" She stopped. "Have a merry Christmas, dear. I'll see you back next term, and we'll start over then, shall we?"

"Yes, ma'am. Merry Christmas," said Julia, and out the door she went.

The December wind followed Julia as she trudged along the empty corridor and up the long flight of stairs to her dormitory. The building was old and its heating just as ancient, and in the winter months the dormitory never lost its frosty chill. Julia pushed open the door, unceremoniously dumped the books she'd been holding onto her trunk, and picked up the blanket folded at the foot of the bed, gathering it around her shoulders.

"What kept you?" asked a voice behind her. Julia turned around and grinned at the sight of her best friend, Lucy, who was stuffing a random assortment of clothing and books into her trunk.

"Bit late for packing?"

"Not at all," said Lucy with a grunt. "Here, sit on this, will you?" Julia parked herself obligingly on top of

the trunk and Lucy snapped the straining catches closed.
A white stocking had escaped from the trunk and was
hanging limply from the side. Lucy chose to ignore it.
"Now: what did Wimpole want?"

Julia flipped her braids back over her shoulders.
"Just wished me a pleasant Christmas, you know," she
said. "Wanted to know about home, and how I was
spending the holiday."

"How *are* you spending Christmas?" asked Lucy.
"I suppose the three terrors will be in attendance?"

"Yes, yes, woe is me!" Julia heaved a dramatic
sigh. "And Father will be home—he's not always able to
be home at Christmas, you know—and it's worse when
he's there because he favors them. Peter and Bertram
will have a row—they always do—and probably Louisa
will try to kill the cat again." She forced a laugh, but
Lucy's brow furrowed.

"I wish you could come home with me. And I
wish it weren't so awful for you."

Julia shrugged. "It's only three weeks. And I've
survived worse."

"Worse than a dead mother and a new family of
thugs?" Julia flinched at the mention of her mother, and
Lucy scooted closer to her on the bed. "I'm sorry," she
said. "That was cruel of me."

Julia shrugged again. "It's hard not to miss her at
Christmas. But there *have* been worse things."

Lucy's eyes narrowed. "What things? What else did you survive? I knew something happened to you last spring—I just knew it. You'd changed when we got back from holidays. You'd … well, you'd grown up all of a sudden."

"Oh, I was visiting my grandparents that week. You remember—we meant to spend the week together in Kent but I was ordered to Oxford instead. I expect it was being around them that did it." She gave a small, hollow laugh.

"No," said Lucy. "I don't mean a change in your speech. You seemed stronger. You know—more confident. Womanly. Something happened; I'm quite certain of it."

On any other day, with any other person, Julia would have flatly denied it. But on this lonely day, a day in which the wind seemed to carry with it a hundred years of secrets, Julia wanted to confide in someone. And here was her very best friend, begging to know. She gathered the blanket closer around her and leaned in closer to Lucy, her eyes sparkling.

"You've got to promise not to tell a soul—not a soul, you understand?"

Lucy nodded, her eyes wide.

"And you've got to promise you'll believe me, no matter how crazy it all sounds. Because it's got to be real, and sometimes I still think it might have all been a dream."

"I promise." Lucy made a cross over her heart.

"All right." Julia took in a deep breath. "That holiday, when I was in Oxford, Peter and I went to another world."

Whatever Lucy had been expecting, it had evidently not been this. She was silent for a long moment, waiting for Julia to say something that was not quite so silly. When Julia didn't speak, Lucy cleared her throat. "You went to … ahem! … where?"

"Another world," repeated Julia. "Like this one, only different. Wilder. It was called Aedyn, and the people who lived there had been enslaved by these three horrible men—beasts, really. Peter and I were called to that world to rescue the people from their slavery. And the three lords and their awful servants almost killed us, but Peter and I led an army against them and we freed the people."

"You freed the people," repeated Lucy.

"Yes," said Julia. "And this monk—his name was Gaius—he told us to keep the whole thing a secret."

"I can't imagine why," said Lucy dryly. Julia ignored her.

"They called me the Deliverer—the Chosen One! And everyone was looking to me for help, but really it *wasn't* me; it was the Lord of Hosts working all the time."

There was a very pregnant pause.

"Julia," Lucy said slowly, "you didn't perhaps have an accident over the holiday?"

"Of course not. You said yourself I seemed grown up."

"Then don't you think perhaps it's time to stop playing silly games?"

Julia felt as if she had been slapped in the face. She blinked hard to keep back the tears that were stinging her eyes. "I wouldn't make up something like this— a world like this. I was there. I saw it. And I know what happened to me."

"You were upset because of your father," said Lucy slowly. "There's no such thing as magic."

"I never *said* it was magic," Julia insisted. "It was the Lord of Hosts, and he has a different kind of power."

Lucy was beginning to become uncomfortable. She nodded and stood up, letting the blanket she'd wrapped around her shoulders fall back onto the bed. "I won't tell anyone," she promised again. "And now don't you think it's time we went down to dinner? We'll be late if we don't hurry."

Julia was crestfallen. She had been so certain that Lucy would believe her. But at least she could look forward to being with Peter over the holiday. He would talk about Aedyn with her. And so she stood and followed Lucy out of the room and down the long flights of stairs to the dining hall to join the other students. And all the while the wind and rain pounded in her ears.

CHAPTER

2

The same rain was falling a few miles north at the King George Academy for Young Men, but Peter, his face being pushed into the mud by a boy much bigger and much stronger than he, paid it no mind. He kicked and flailed as he tried to knock the older boy off his balance, rage giving him a strength he didn't usually possess. With an arm taut with muscle Peter beat back the hand that was holding him down and sprang to his feet. Before his opponent could react Peter had planted a fist hard in his face, and a bright ribbon of blood gushed from his nose.

The crowd that had been taunting Peter broke into cheers as the older boy stumbled back. Peter stood

still, catching his breath and ignoring the shouts, waiting in case another fist should come his way. But a hand
came down on his shoulder first: Professor Boldly.

"You'll be coming with me, Mr. Grant," he was
saying. "The rest of you, be off!"

The ring of boys that had surrounded the fight
broke up and scattered. The older boy, Mason, was
on his knees now, holding both hands to his nose and
whimpering. Peter watched as he looked up to see if
Boldly was noticing. He wasn't, and Mason whimpered
all the louder.

"Up to the infirmary with you, Mason," Boldly said, marching Peter away. His big hand stayed firmly on Peter's shoulder as they marched back up to the school. The rain had turned the snowy field to mud, and they were both soaked through and covered in splatters by the time they reached the building. This state of affairs did not seem to improve Boldly's mood.

"Fourth time this term," he was saying, giving Peter's shoulder a shake with every step he took. "Never have I seen … never, in all my years of teaching …" His heels clicked on the stone floor as he dragged Peter, who was half shuffling and half running to keep up.

They stopped in front of a closed door. Boldly knocked on it sharply and waited until a low voice murmured, "Enter."

The door creaked open. A very fat man with a most impressive mustache sat before him, swathed in voluminous black robes. He folded his hands over his stomach and peered over his spectacles at the man and boy in front of him.

"Ah, Mr. Grant," he breathed. "So we find ourselves here once again." He nodded a dismissal to Boldly, who gave Peter's shoulder a final, vicious shake and stalked from the room. The clicking of his heels echoed in the corridor for a long, empty moment.

"And what have you to say for yourself this time?" asked the headmaster once the clicking had faded.

"It was Mason, sir," said Peter. "He was talking about the archery tournament next week, and he said I was a weakling and I'd lose it for the house, and he supposed my dead mother taught me to shoot."

"Ah," said the headmaster. "And you found this sufficient reason to hit him? Not very sportsmanlike, Mr. Grant."

"He hit me first," said Peter quickly.

"I think we both know that's not the case," the headmaster replied. He sat back in his chair, which gave a long, protesting creak, and removed his spectacles. He rubbed his temple with his thumb and forefinger and gave a tired sigh. "As this is the third—no, fourth, is it?—incident this term, we'll be alerting the Captain to your conduct. This behavior simply will not be tolerated. Is this understood, Mr. Grant?"

Peter nodded. "Yes, sir."

"Good." The headmaster replaced his spectacles on his nose. "Off with you. Perhaps the Captain will beat some sense into you over the holiday."

Peter scurried out of the office and closed the door behind him. Leaning against the wall outside the headmaster's office he wiped a hand over his face, trying to scratch away some of the mud that was already drying on his cheek. Mason was a bully and a wretch. He'd get away with murder if he wanted, and all because his father was on the board. Wonderful Mason, perfect Mason would never provoke a fight. And now Peter's father would know.

Peter took a deep breath, dreading the punishment that he knew was waiting for him at home. In the old days he would have gotten a lecture and that would have been the end of it—in the days before Bertram and Louisa and the Wicked Stepmother. But now it would be worse. Much worse.

Julia heard the shouting as soon as she opened the door. Her shoulders dropped as she heard Peter's name from the other room—something about bringing disgrace on the family name. Something about sportsmanship and controlling one's temper. Something about teaching him a lesson. She wanted to drop her bags there and run for her room—run someplace where she couldn't hear this frightening man who no longer sounded like her father.

Before she could flee the scene, however, there were footsteps on the stairs, and Julia looked up to see a girl about her age coming down, her pinched face twisted into a decidedly self-satisfied smirk as she hummed quietly to herself. Her mouse-brown hair was pulled back into two tight braids, and her beady gray eyes were frozen into a squint. Louisa.

"Look who's back," she said, her nasal humming ceasing. "Silly little Julia, the girl nobody ever loved, home in time for Christmas."

Julia had a profound desire to pull one of Louisa's stringy braids.

"What's going on in there?" she asked, nodding toward her father's study door.

"Oh, didn't you hear? Peter got in another fight at school. The headmaster sent a letter. Says if it happens again he'll be expelled."

There came the sound of a strike, and then a muffled yell. Julia's face went white as Louisa's smirk broadened into a grin. "Mother says he's totally out of control and ought to be sent to a special school for hopeless cases."

"Indeed." A tall, angular woman appeared on the stairs, and Julia looked up at the sound of her stepmother's voice. Her dark hair was pulled back tight from her scalp into a tiny bun, and the harsh lines of her dress only emphasized the severity of her face. Her stepmother's lips forced themselves into a thin smile. "Welcome home, Julia. Let us hope that you've been conducting yourself in a more suitable fashion than your brother."

"Yes, ma'am."

"Good then. Take your things up to your room and change into something"—her nose wrinkled as she regarded Julia's wilted traveling clothes—"more appropriate for a young lady. Supper in an hour." She smiled that thin smile again and Julia went up the stairs to her room, trying not to listen to the hushed sobs coming from her father's study.

"I don't want you spending much time around either of them, darling," her stepmother was saying in a tone that was not at all hushed—so loud, in fact, that Julia was sure she was meant to hear. "They're an appalling influence on you and Bertie. Their mother must have been a dreadful woman."

There was no supper for Peter that evening, and it wasn't until after she was sent to bed that Julia was able to sneak into his room to see him. He was sitting up in bed, a book open on his knees. There was a hard, bitter look on his face, but it softened when he saw his sister. She parked herself at the foot of his bed.

"I'm sorry," she said. "Father was horrible."

Peter shrugged. "I thought it would be different. You know, after Aedyn, after all we went through there—I thought it would be easier to be in school and handle Father and ... I just thought it would be different."

"So did I."

"We defeated the Jackal, the Leopard, and the Wolf. You'd think I could handle the headmaster."

"Or at least Bertram and Louisa." Julia grinned, and at the sight of it Peter gave a low laugh.

"Good old Bertie. We'll have some fun with him this holiday, eh? Oh …" Peter hopped off the bed and retrieved his schoolbag, which lay still unpacked just inside the door. He opened the satchel and took out a small package wrapped up in brown paper and string. "Here." He held out the package to Julia. "Got this for you. Merry Christmas."

Julia took the package from his hand and untied the string carefully. She peeled apart the wrapping to reveal a worn, leather-bound book. *Alice in Wonderland*. She looked up at Peter in surprise.

"Because you were right, you know. About dreams and other worlds and all that." And then it was Peter's turn to be surprised as Julia threw her arms around him.

CHAPTER

3

Christmas was wretched, of course. That morning
Peter and Julia had woken to find a new, clean
blanket of snow covering the house, the trees,
and the yard, and they both felt the tingle of anticipation
that arrives on such a morning. But it didn't last long.

They went downstairs to find their father, their
stepmother, and Bertram and Louisa all sitting around
the tree drinking hot chocolate and laughing together
just like—well, just like a real family, Julia thought. The
two children had already picked out which presents
they wanted to open first.

Louisa got a dollhouse and Bertram got a new
fishing rod and tackle box, complete with its own set
of lures—"So that we can fish together in the spring,"

the Captain said. Julia got a dress that she strongly believed was a hand-me-down from Louisa (judging by
the smirk) and a pendant from her grandmother. It was
carved out of some sort of greenish stone and shaped
like a star with six long points. It hung on a thin gold
chain and was accompanied by a short note:

> *I found this by the pond in our garden, Julia*
> *dear. I can't think where it came from, but it*
> *seemed that it would suit you. A most unusual*
> *pendant, but I do hope you like it. Much love*
> *and a very merry Christmas to you.*

Julia held the pendant in the hot palm of her
hand. Something felt familiar about it—something that
she couldn't quite put her finger on. She fastened the
chain around her throat and tucked the pendant into
the high collar of her nightgown. The stone was cool
against her skin.

Peter received a worn velvet box from his father.
It opened on a hinge to reveal a tarnished compass that
had seen better days.

"That compass has weathered many a storm with
me," said the Captain. "I hope it will remind you to steer
your course in life straight."

Peter and Julia's stepmother murmured her
agreement. "Your father's right. You need some sense of
direction."

Peter looked at his father, looked at his compass, and then looked at Bertram's new fishing rod. "Thank you, Father," he said, and then shoved the box in the pocket of his bathrobe and tried very hard to forget all about it.

After they had opened their gifts the children all went upstairs to change for Christmas dinner. Julia took off the necklace and put on her new dress, twisting and turning in front of the mirror to see how it looked. It didn't fit right—too big in the waist and stretched too tight around the shoulders. Definitely Louisa's. But her father smiled when he saw it and said, "There's my girl." It was the first time he'd said this to her since he remarried, and she went into his arms for an embrace. He held her strong and close, and she breathed in the familiar scent of tobacco and aftershave.

"Do you"—she paused, not wanting to ruin the moment. "Do you ever miss Mother?"

She listened to her father breathe—once, twice, three times. "Of course I do. I miss her every day."

Julia tightened her arms around his waist, pressing her cheek against the buttons of his shirt. "Me too," she said.

"But now you've got Louisa to play with, darling, and we're a whole family again." Julia stiffened, pulling away from her father. "And that's the best Christmas present of all, don't you think?"

She forced a smile. "Yes, Father. Best it could be."

The Captain patted her shoulder. "Run along now and tell Cook we'll be ready in a minute. Plum pudding, darling ... won't it be lovely?"

"Just lovely, Father."

It wasn't lovely. Peter was in a rotten mood and sat sullenly in his seat at the table, picking at the roast and mashing the peas with his fork. Julia was quiet because Peter was quiet, and Bertram—horrid Bertram— filled in the silence with a long story about how he'd gotten some other boy in trouble at school.

"He'd been sniveling in the baths during the science lecture," Bertram was saying, "and I told Professor Rotswort he was there, and you should have seen him when he came out! He was all red and blubbering, and he got a beating for skipping class."

"How very sportsmanlike of you," Peter said, and the table went silent. Julia found herself clenching her fist around her knife. Her knuckles had gone white.

"Young men," said the Captain, taking a long sip of wine from his glass, "who do not know the meaning of fair play ought not to lecture those who do." His eyes moved from the wine in the bottom of his glass to his son's ashen face. "Apologize, Peter."

Peter pushed back his chair from the table. He stood. He picked up his glass of water. And he flung it straight into Bertram's fat face.

It was a few hours later that Julia found herself once again knocking on Peter's door. After several knocks there was still no answer.

"It's just me," she said against the door. "I brought some things from the kitchen." She heard a grunt on the other side and thought it sufficient permission to enter.

Peter was standing by the bed, stuffing a bundle of clothing into a sack. He was wearing a hat and boots, and his winter overcoat lay unbuttoned over his shoulders. A scarf and pair of gloves—nice leather gloves, probably Bertram's—lay beside the sack.

Julia took it all in with a moment's glance. "Where are you going?" she asked.

"Away," said Peter. "To Oxford, maybe. Grandmother and Grandfather would understand."

Julia set the plate of sandwiches she'd brought from the kitchen on Peter's dresser. She thought for a moment. "Can I come with you?"

"Of course not. You'd only slow me up." Peter folded a navy blue sweater into a clumsy square and shoved aside the other contents of his sack to make room for it.

"I wouldn't," said Julia. "You think I want to stay here a minute longer? They're just as awful to me—especially since they think you tried to drown

Bertram. Let me come, Peter." He shook his head and resumed his packing, but Julia grabbed his coat and turned him around to face her. "I'm coming. I'll meet you out back in ten minutes — just give me ten minutes, all right?"

Peter started to speak but then stopped, his mouth hanging open. He nodded toward the plate of sandwiches she'd left on the dresser. "Don't forget to wrap those up. We might get hungry on the way."

Twelve minutes later (it had taken her the extra two minutes to wrap up the sandwiches, Julia said) they met by the back door of the house. Julia was bundled up in several layers of scarves and had her ice skates tied to her bag by their laces.

"Skates?" said Peter.

"For the pond in Oxford," said Julia.

"Ah," said Peter. And they were off.

They had to cross a long stretch of lawn before they hit the trees that lined the drive, and Julia spent the walk hoping that no one would think to look out the window just then and see them running away. In this she was not so fortunate, but it would be a few minutes yet before she found this out. Peter had his compass out and was insisting that the shortest path to the train station was, in fact, through the woods.

"I don't care," Julia said. "We'll lose the way if we don't go by the road. You remember how hard it was to find our way through those forests in Aedyn? We ought to have gotten lost a hundred times."

"But we'll be seen if we go by the road," said Peter. "Come on. North by northeast." He plunged into the woods, and Julia had little choice but to follow.

It soon became clear that they should have left a few hours earlier if they were going to leave at all, for the night was just beginning to press against the sky and the branches of the trees above them were starting to cast long shadows over the snow. They walked quickly, not talking much. Peter checked the compass from time to time, sometimes changing direction slightly to stay perfectly on course, and Julia followed behind him, tramping in his larger footsteps.

It couldn't have been ten minutes since they had reached the woods — though it felt much longer indeed — when they came to the stream. It was swollen with the melted ice and rain from the storm, and rushing much faster than they had last seen it in the summer. Peter paused, uncertain how to proceed, and checked his compass again. There was no way to jump the stream now.

"Oh, honestly," said Julia. "You know we'll never get across it like this."

"If it were only a bit colder I suppose you could jolly well skate across!" said Peter shortly.

"I don't suppose it gets any narrower if we follow it for a bit ..."

"No. It'll be worse further on. This is the only place you can jump—don't you remember? We used to do it back when we were kids." Peter turned the compass to one side, perhaps hoping it would tell a different story.

"Then I suppose we go back to the road."

"No, we'll be seen. I already told you."

Julia put her hands on her hips and raised her chin in a way that befit the Chosen One of Aedyn, and probably Peter would have relented had he been given the chance. In fact, he had already opened his mouth to say "All right, have it your way," but another voice—a thin, nasal voice—came first.

"Naughty naughty, trying to run away! Wait until your papa hears." It was Louisa, standing a ways back from them and half hidden in the trees. Peter's heart plummeted into his stomach. She was going to ruin everything. Everything.

"Go away, Louisa," said Julia sternly, her pointed chin still raised. "You're not wanted here. Go back home and tattle on us like the little beast you are."

"And if I do they'll know right where to find you," taunted Louisa. Peter and Julia looked down: she was right. Their tracks were laid out in the snow, plain as day for anyone to follow. Louisa put her hands behind her back and started humming—she was always humming, thought Julia.

"Next time," Peter said to his sister, "remind me to run away in the summer." And remembering the strength that had come to his fingers when he held the bow and arrow and faced the dark lords of Aedyn, Peter knelt down, scooped up an icy fistful of snow, packed it into a ball, and hurled it at Louisa.

She shrieked and threw up her hands, but not quickly enough, and the snowball smacked right into her nose. Peter laughed and launched another, then another, until Louisa started to run. And he really cannot be blamed that she had lost her bearing and ran toward the stream, and not back in the direction from which she had come.

Water that has just been frozen has not forgotten its chill, and Louisa screamed as it closed over her. Julia found that she was screaming too, and she and Peter both rushed forward to help her. But as they raced to the water they found that they were standing not on the bank of a stream but on the edge of an icy chasm, and before they could cry out they were both falling in.

CHAPTER

G et off! Get *off* of me!"
Peter came to his senses and rolled over
onto his side. A gasping, spluttering Louisa lay
on her back, her perpetual smirk replaced by a look of
stark terror.

"What … you … where did you take me? What
did you *do?*" She was practically screeching.

"*I* didn't do anything. *You* followed us and then
you ran the wrong way and we had to rescue you."

"Some rescue! What is this place, anyway?"

Peter looked around. They were inside a massive
stone room. Chandeliers hung from a ceiling far above
their heads and elaborate stonework covered the walls.
He looked about for Julia and found her collapsed at the

far end of the room. As he watched she propped herself up and stood, looking out a small window. She turned to face them, and Peter recognized the smile on her face.

"We're back," she said simply. "We've made it back."

"Made it back *where?*"

"Oh, do be quiet," Peter snapped at Louisa. He hopped up and went over to the window, standing beside Julia. The window was long and narrow, but they were high up and he could see a long way, over rolling hills and valleys, all of it lush and green and just as he remembered it. He breathed in deeply, letting the air of Aedyn fill his lungs, and for the first time in a long time he felt that he was home.

"It's all so quiet," said Julia, and with a start Peter realized that it was. They were in the Great Hall of the Citadel of Aedyn—there was the dais where the three thrones of the Lords of Aedyn had sat, and there was the blackened spot on the floor where he had shown them how to use gunpowder—but there was none of the ordinary noise and bustle that one would expect to hear in a castle. No servants going about their duties, no clomping of heavy footsteps on the stone floors.

"What's going *on?*" whined Louisa behind them. Peter stifled a low groan, and Julia turned and went over to her. She put out a hand and helped her to her feet. "We're in a place called Aedyn. It's a different kind of world, and I think we must have been called here. Peter and I have been here before, so you're just going to have to trust us, all right?"

"But how do we get home?" Louisa wailed. Julia stopped herself in the middle of rolling her eyes and tried to speak patiently.

"I don't know yet. First we have to figure out why we're here." She turned her head to look at Peter. "Right?"

"Right. And we start by figuring out where all the people have gone." He walked toward the big oak doors at the opposite end of the Great Hall and, with a great deal of pushing and grunting, heaved them open. "Follow me, ladies," he said.

The rest of the castle was just as empty as the Hall. There were no signs of a great struggle, and the place did not seem to have been long abandoned. There was no dust on the window ledges or chairs, and all the furnishings were perfectly in order. Indeed, it seemed as if the castle's occupants had simply vanished.

Julia and Louisa followed Peter down a long corridor lined with tapestries. At the end of the corridor he pushed open another door—this one not nearly as heavy and ornate as the entrance to the Great Hall. The three children entered a room warmly lit by the afternoon sun. Huge legs of cured meat hung from the ceiling and pots and pans lined the walls. Long tables fairly groaned under the weight of bulging sacks and heavy bowls. The fire in the grate seemed to have burned out some time ago, but a big black pot full of some kind of soup hung suspended from a chain above the ashes.

"We might as well get something to eat," suggested Julia. "We don't know what we'll find out there—and it may be some time before we have a decent meal again. Remember last time, Peter?"

He gave a rueful grin. He did indeed remember. Upon their arrival in Aedyn they had found themselves without food or water for most of a day, and it was not

a day he would care to repeat. "Agreed. Let's take anything we can carry. Julia, see if you can find some skins
for water, and Louisa, you take some of that sausage." He
gestured at a long string of links that was hanging near
her head. "Here, put it in this," he said, and threw his
satchel at her. She caught it and looked at him.

"Why should I?"

"Because if you don't we'll leave you here all
alone forever," said Peter. "Get to work." She stared at
him blankly for a moment, then pulled down the string
of sausages and started gathering it into the satchel.
Peter thought she might be about to cry, but instead she
began to hum in her thin voice. Except her voice wasn't
as thin as it had been at home, and whatever melody she
was humming wasn't quite so tuneless.

Julia, meanwhile, had found some wineskins and
was starting to work the long arm of the water pump in
the corner of the kitchen. Up and down it went, up and
down. She motioned to Peter, and he came over to hold
the skins under the steady stream of water. "You don't
have to be so beastly to her, you know," Julia said under
her breath.

"Me? Beastly?"

"You know what I mean," said Julia, her eyebrows furrowed as she concentrated on her task. "She's
a spoiled wretch but it won't be easy on her, being here.
The least we can do is be decent to her."

"Decent? When was the last time she was decent to either of us?"

"Never. But that doesn't mean we can't show her a little kindness."

Peter glanced over at his stepsister. "I suppose not," he said. The skin was full to bursting, and Peter pulled it out from under the stream, tied off the neck tightly, and thrust the next one under the pump. "Does seem rotten luck, though. We finally get back here and we have to bring her along with us."

"I know." Julia shrugged her shoulders and stopped pumping. The water slowed to a trickle—just enough for Peter to fill the last skin. He tied the neck of this skin as well.

"Are you done with the sausages?" he asked Louisa.

"Done." She'd slung the satchel over her shoulder. "And now will you tell me where we're going?"

"That's what we're trying to find out," said Peter. "Here"—he flung open a cupboard door and peered inside. "There's bread and cheese in this cupboard." He took out two hard loaves and a wheel of cheese and slid them over the counter to Louisa. "Carry those too, will you?"

They exited the kitchen the same way they'd come and left the castle by way of a twisting, turning road that went down through the village and out into a green meadow. What Peter and Julia remembered as little more than a deer trail was now a heavily traversed lane leading ... Peter pulled the compass out of his pocket and flicked it open with his thumb. South. The lane must be leading them down to the sea.

Julia, walking beside him, was positively gleeful. It was strange to be called here again, certainly, but the tingling in her fingertips told her that an adventure was at hand. And whatever dangers might lie ahead, she was free of school and grades and horrid Bertram and horrider ...

The contented sounds of munching that came from behind reminded Julia that she and Peter were not alone on this adventure. She turned and saw that Louisa had already seen fit to break into one of the hard loaves of bread. She had broken off a large chunk and was carrying it in her fist, gnawing off big bites as she walked.

"You *did* just have Christmas dinner a few hours ago," Julia reminded her. "And we might need that bread before long."

"Need it for what?" Louisa asked, her mouth still half full of crumbs. "I thought we were trying to get home. Aren't we going home?"

"Eventually, I suppose," said Julia. "But before we do we need to find out why we were called here in the first place."

"We'll be whipped for being out so long." Louisa tore off another chunk of bread with her teeth. "At least the two of you will. I'll tell Mummy that you made me come along and you promised me sweets and then you left me out in the woods. And then she'll send you both to that special school for horrid children and you'll never be allowed to come home on holidays ever again."

Peter was about to say something particularly nasty—Julia could see it in his face—but before he could open his mouth the three of them heard a very different sort of sound indeed. It was a woman's scream, high and loud. And it was coming from just over the ridge.

CHAPTER

5

Peter and Julia didn't need to look at each other. They were both running, running as fast their legs could carry them, running with all their strength toward the beach and toward the sound of that scream.

Louisa fell behind almost at once. She had never been an athlete and didn't have Julia and Peter's endurance, besides which she was still chewing and hampered with the satchel of food. When she finally caught up, red-faced and breathless, the satchel slapping against her side, Peter and Julia were crouched behind a grouping of bushes, whispering and pointing at something she couldn't see.

"What *is* it?" Louisa asked. She threw down the satchel and peered over the bushes at the crest of the ridge. They were standing at the top of a dune that went down to a sparkling sea, and there was a ship on the sea … but that was all she saw before Peter pulled her down roughly into the long grass.

"Stay *down!*" he hissed. "We can't be seen—don't you understand that?"

"But maybe someone down there will know how to get …"

"*Quiet!*"

Louisa closed her mouth, sat down roughly on the ground, and began to cry. Peter gave her a withering look, resisting the strong urge to kick her, and went back to spying on the beach.

"Just there—no, there," said Julia, pointing. "See? The woman who screamed—she must be with them." Peter nodded. A longboat had just pushed off from the beach, and in it they could just make out a few bedraggled figures being rowed out to sea by six uniformed guards. "But where are they going?"

"Look," said Peter. Julia cast her eyes over the horizon and saw a schooner anchored out in the deep water. It was riding high in the water, its sails billowing out from three enormous masts. The longboat nearest shore was one of a dozen that were rowing steadily toward it, all of them full of the same guards and their bedraggled prisoners.

"What will we do?"

"Do? We'll go home—home to Mummy and ... and Bertie!" Louisa was blubbering helplessly on the tall grasses behind the bushes.

Peter raised an eyebrow at his sister. "We should have left her at the castle," he muttered.

Julia chose to ignore him. "Those guards, taking all the people ... why are they taking the people?"

"I don't know," Peter replied. "But I'll bet that's why we were brought here."

Julia nodded, her eyes still fixed on the schooner. "But how do we find out where they're going? Unless they happened to leave a boat behind we can't very well follow."

Peter's eyes scanned the shoreline. "There are some reeds down there. We'll cut them up and swim, breathing through the tubes. It'll be like snorkeling!"

"Very clever, Peter. And if we should get tired, or if we can't keep up with the ship?"

"Ah. I see the difficulty." The longboats had almost all reached the schooner now, and Peter and Julia watched from a distance as the prisoners were boarded onto the ship. People they had known, perhaps, or the children of those they had known. It was a long, slow process—the prisoners did not seem particularly eager to board the schooner—and only one of them at a time could climb up the flimsy rope ladder. But finally it was done, and one by one the longboats were hoisted back onto the schooner.

"We should go down to the beach," said Peter. "See if they left … anything." Julia nodded and rose. Louisa was still blubbering.

"Louisa, we don't have time for this," Julia said sternly. "Some friends of ours are in trouble, and we need to help them, and if you stop crying you can help them too." Louisa looked out from between the fingers she'd been sobbing into.

"All right," she said.

Perhaps you have once had some occasion to run down a dune—during a family holiday at the beach, perhaps. If so, you will understand the exquisite pleasure that comes from the sensation of tripping and falling as you run, the hot sand squeezing between your toes as you fight to stay upright. You know the ecstasy of tumbling over and over, your feet never quite catching up to each other, until you collapse at the bottom.

Peter, Julia, and Louisa did not have such an experience as they descended the dune. They were trying to be careful, and they were trying to be quiet, and most of all Julia and Peter were trying to keep Louisa from hurting herself and starting to cry again. It was, Peter muttered to himself, just like having a child hanging about.

There was nothing to be seen on the beach. No prisoners, no guards, no longboats, and nothing that would give them a clue as to where the invaders had come from and where they were taking their prisoners. A few footprints on the beach, and that was all. Peter kicked his right foot savagely and a spray of sand burst up into the air. A dead end.

"I wish Gaius were here," Julia said, looking out at the schooner. It had hoisted its anchor and was turning toward the horizon, its billowing sails filling with wind. "Should we go to the garden, do you think?"

"What garden?" asked Louisa. She looked positively overwhelmed, and Julia began to feel a bit sorry
for her. It was worse for Louisa, Julia thought. She didn't
know anything about this place, and here she was thrust
into the middle of everything.

"The King's Garden," Julia said. "It's a place sa-
cred to the Lord of Hosts, and if we go there we might
find some clue about all of this."

"Lord of Hosts?" Louisa asked, bewildered.

"He's—well, he's the one in charge around here,"
Julia explained. "We can't see him, but he's watching
over everything, and I think he must have been the one
who called us."

"Come on," said Peter. "Let's go the garden.
Things usually tend to happen there."

The garden wasn't far from the beach, and the
path through the woods had been cleared since last
they'd walked it. The terrain was level and there was
a sweet breeze whistling through the leaves, and had it
not been for Louisa the walk might have been pleasant
indeed. For they couldn't have been ten minutes into
the journey when she started to complain.

The sun was too hot, the ground was too hard,
the birds were too loud, the bag was too heavy. At this
last Peter valiantly took the satchel of food, finding it no-
ticeably lighter than it had been when first packed. But

a moment later Louisa decided that she'd been walking too long. She sat down against a tree and began to cry.

"I think we should leave her here," Peter told Julia unsympathetically. "We'll never make it to the garden at this rate, and she'll be safe until we can come back for her."

Julia was, truth be told, inclined to agree, but she shook her head. "You know we can't just abandon her. And besides, we'll all be safest in the garden. It's not far." She went to her stepsister and put out a hand to help her up. "It's not far, Louisa," she said again.

And indeed it wasn't long before they came to the garden. The familiar silver glow welcomed them in, but once inside its borders Peter and Julia found that the garden was, as it had been the first time they'd seen it, badly overgrown. Vines and weeds had grown wild and untended, strangling the buds of flowers that had once bloomed there and choking off the life of the garden in their thorns. The great fountain in the center of the garden had run dry, the stone basin encrusted in mosses and lichens. Peter and Julia felt that they had stumbled upon an ancient ruin, long neglected, its purpose all but forgotten.

"This is it?" said Louisa. "*This* is your precious garden?"

Julia was too upset to answer. Peter shuffled his feet on the ground, kicking aside a mess of vines. "It didn't look like this when we left," he said. "It's been left to rot. I can't think …"

And just at that moment something rather extraordinary happened.

There was a sound above them in the sky—the sound of the beating of massive wings. Peter, Julia, and Louisa looked up to see a dark blur which quickly took on the shape of a bird—a falcon, Peter said under his breath. It pulled its wings tight into its body and plummeted toward them, landing with a dull thud near the stone throne at the other end of the garden.

All three of the children had gone absolutely white with terror as the bird came down, for it was like no falcon they had ever seen. It was absolutely enormous—the size of the dragons in fairy stories, Julia thought with a start. Each of its golden eyes were the size of the children's entire heads, and one snap of that enormous beak could have broken their backs.

"Back up," said Peter slowly, never breaking his gaze with the falcon's eye. "Slowly. Into the trees." Evidently even Louisa knew that this was a time to be silent, for she obeyed without the usual protesting and weeping.

The bird saw that they were moving and twitched its head to the side. It beat its wings once, and the children could feel the rush of air on their faces.

"Do we run?" asked Julia in a low breath, and Peter was about to answer when the falcon lifted its head, opened its beak, and let out a terrible screech. And Peter and Julia would have run—would have run until the breath left their bodies—had Louisa not chosen precisely that moment to faint dead away.

CHAPTER

The falcon was coming toward them, its mighty talons crunching into the earth with every step it took. Julia fell to her knees and began shaking and slapping Louisa with all her might, desperate to rouse her and run away, run anywhere.

"We'll have to carry her," Peter hissed, but it was already too late. Julia felt the darkness of a shadow overhead, and she looked up to see that the falcon was upon them.

It bent its head down so that it was level with them, and Peter stood tall, taller than he had ever stood when facing his father, staring straight into that cold golden eye. Julia could see that he was quivering and his face had gone absolutely white, but his gaze did not waver. And as he stood and waited, the falcon turned its neck once again and brushed the top of its head against Peter's cheek.

Peter gasped and staggered back as if he'd been struck, stumbling back onto the grass, but then he looked up at the falcon and thought maybe, just maybe, that it seemed to be waiting for him. He reached out a hand and—slowly—carefully—touched the crest of its head, just behind the eyes.

The falcon let out a sound that might, in a cat, have been described as a purr. It opened its beak and let out a series of short squawks. Peter reached out his hand again and stroked it harder this time, running his fingers through the dark feathers.

"Careful," whispered Julia in the softest breath she could manage. Peter shook his head, his gaze still locked with the falcon's, as he ran his hand over the bird's head and neck, and then all the way down along its wing.

"It's all right," Peter said. "I think it's all right."

The falcon squawked again and bobbed its head up and down, then shuffled its feet back and bent down so that its back was level with Peter's shoulders. Peter ran his hand along the length of its back, stopping just

before the long tail feathers. "I think we're meant to ride him," he said.

Before Julia had time to protest Peter threw his arm over the top of the falcon's wing and scrambled up onto its back, his feet jostling to get a foothold. Finally he was perched triumphantly on top of the falcon, swaying a bit as the bird adjusted its position, and he grinned down at Julia.

"Nothing to it," he said. "Climb on up!"

"I don't ... Peter, I don't think that's such a good idea." Julia's gaze was still locked on that sharp beak. But he reached his hand down to her and hoisted her up, and before she knew it she was sitting behind Peter with her arms tight around his waist, wondering if that beak could still reach them back here.

"It's all right," Peter said again. "We were meant to come here to the garden—you were right! The Lord of Hosts must have sent the falcon. It's better than a ship. We can ride him all the way to—to wherever those ships are headed."

Julia's only response was a tightening of her grip around Peter's waist. Defeating dark lords was one thing, but flying up over the sea? What did the Lord of Hosts expect of them?

The falcon rose to its feet, and Peter and Julia found themselves swaying on its back as they struggled to find a grip. Julia looked down. The ground seemed very, very far away. And then she gave a little cry, for Louisa was still crumpled in a heap where she'd fallen.

"Louisa! Peter, Louisa's still down there! We need to get her up here ..." But just as she spoke, the falcon picked Louisa up in one of his great claws, beat its wings twice, and rose into the air.

Julia screamed as they mounted into the air and grabbed at anything she could hold onto—Peter, mostly. Peter had crouched low as they ascended above the trees, and then, seeing where they were going, he threw out his arms and broke into a yell.

All of Aedyn was laid out before them. Looking around, Peter was able to see the castle, and the garden, and suddenly all the trees became a great mass of green forest. The coastline approached, and Peter could see the harbors and inlets and rivers that came in from the sea.

They flew over the dune and the beach and then they were at sea. The air changed—it was colder, with the salt spray hovering above the waves, and it must have been this that stirred Louisa out of her faint. Peter and Julia, riding low over the falcon's back, felt the bird shift its position in the air. And then they heard a familiar scream.

There were no words in it yet—just a long, high-pitched shriek. The falcon was getting its balance, adjusting to the writhing girl in its talons. Julia stuck her head over the edge as far as she dared and could just see the edges of Louisa's braids flinging themselves out from her head.

"It's all right!" Julia cried. "Hush, Louisa! It's safe!" But if Louisa heard her there was no indication, and it was a long, long time before the screaming stopped. After a time it was replaced by a dull whimper and the occasional sob, and bothersome as it was for the two children riding on the falcon's back, even Peter had to admit that riding in a giant falcon's claws could not be the most comfortable way to travel.

They rode over a quiet sea, the salt breeze in their hair and the sun high above them. Foam-tipped waves crested beneath them, and a few brave seagulls scavenged the rocks over which they broke. There was no land on the horizon, just more water and more waves, but occasionally Peter and Julia caught a glimpse of the schooner that they were following. The falcon stayed far away from it—perhaps it understood that they had to stay out of sight.

"Where do you think it's taking us?" asked Julia. She had to shout—the wind rushing around and above them almost took her words away with it.

"Don't know," Peter yelled back. "The nearest land is Khemia, but there couldn't be anything left there. No people, at least. Not after the volcano erupted and everyone fled."

This exchange was met by a renewed whimpering from Louisa.

The falcon moved through the air swiftly and steadily, as if the very breath of the Lord of Hosts was at its back, but it was a long, long time before Peter and Julia saw anything on the horizon other than water. The sun began to sink low in the sky, and with it the air burst into a kaleidoscope of oranges and purples. And in the moment that the sun slipped below the horizon, in that magical moment when it is not quite day and not quite night, Peter felt Julia slump against his back and loosen her hold on his waist. She had fallen asleep.

He leaned forward and gripped the falcon's neck all the tighter, and though it did not make a sound, Peter felt warm and comforted all through his body. The twilight faded into night, and one by one the familiar stars of Aedyn winked into the sky. Peter looked up at them and breathed a prayer to the One who had called them, though he did not even know what to pray. He lay there for what seemed like hours, awake and yet not awake, feeling the warm body soaring beneath him, watching the winking of the stars and waiting for what would come.

CHAPTER

7

Dawn had just begun to touch the sky when Peter began to feel a change in the bird's flight. It had tucked its wings in closer to its body and was beginning, he felt instinctively, to descend. He reached behind him and touched Julia's leg, shaking it just enough to rouse her. She sat up straight and yawned, removing a hand from her brother's waist to rub her eyes.

"Are we—oh," she said. "Still on the bird, are we?"

"Afraid so," said Peter. "But something's beginning to happen, I think. Look." He pointed to a spot just below the horizon, and Julia could make out a flock of birds swarming above the waves. Gulls. "They wouldn't come this far out to sea unless there were land nearby," said Peter. A sudden inspiration striking him, Peter reached into his pocket and retrieved the compass he had been given by his father. He flicked open the top and squinted in the dim morning light. "North," he said. "North by northeast. What's north of Aedyn?"

"Khemia," said Julia. "It must be Khemia."

They watched silently as the sky began to brighten. Peter's eyelids were heavy and might have begun to droop had they not seen something new on the horizon: a huge bank of clouds, tinted red by the dawn. As they drew closer they could see the jagged tip of a mountain jutting through the clouds like a knife.

The falcon banked to the left as they approached, beginning a steep descent that brought a new round of screaming from the direction of its talons. Peter held tight to its neck and Julia held tight to Peter as they fell from the sky. They seemed to be heading straight for a forest—straight into the trees. Julia squeezed her eyes shut and screamed straight into Peter's ear, quite certain that they were about to crash. She felt the rushing of leaves and twigs around her and was shaken by a *thump!* as the falcon landed, and she and Peter tumbled off its back onto soft, cool sand. Louisa lay a few feet away in a clump of reeds—it looked as though she'd been dropped just before the falcon landed. She had fainted again. Seeing her stepsister collapsed in a heap on the ground, Julia breathed a sigh of relief. At least she wasn't screaming ... for now.

Peter had tumbled onto his stomach in the sand, and he raised himself to his feet to have a look around. The place seemed deserted enough: a natural harbor, close to the sea and surrounded by a grove of trees. They could conceal themselves quite easily here if the need arose. He stretched his arms above his head, then reached out a hand to help Julia to her feet.

"I suppose we ought to try to wake her," said Peter grimly, nodding in Louisa's direction.

"It's been rotten for her," Julia agreed, and picked her way through the reeds to the water's edge. She peered carefully in both directions. There was no one in sight, and she cupped her hands together and bent to scoop up a handful of water. She trod carefully back the way she had come and dumped the water unceremoniously all over her stepsister's face.

Louisa woke with a splutter and a gasp. Peter, seeing that she was likely to start screaming again, clapped a hand tight over her mouth. "Now look here," he said, teeth clenched. "I'll take my hand away if you promise to be quiet — very quiet. We don't know exactly where we are and we don't know who our friends or enemies are, so we need to stay hidden, and most important of all you are not to scream. Understand? You have to be very, very quiet."

Louisa nodded beneath his grip, and Peter took his hand away. "Very quiet," he said again, and Louisa pushed herself up and wiped a hand across her eyes. She'd been crying.

"I didn't want to come here," she said. "I never wanted to come to this beastly place. I only wanted to see where you were running to."

"You were trying to get us in trouble," Julia corrected, but Louisa ignored her and went on.

"And you brought me here, not a soul for miles, no one who knows how to get me home, and maybe enemies, and that horrid bird taking me all across an ocean in its claws—oh it's awful, just awful!" And she began to cry again. They were not, it must be noted, quiet tears.

Peter heaved a world-weary sigh and looked over at the falcon, who had been waiting very patiently at the edge of the clearing. It had cocked its head and was watching Louisa in a curious manner. It opened its beak and gave another one of its shrill, screeching squawks.

"I wish it could talk," Julia said. "I wonder what it might tell us about all of this."

"Nothing!" sobbed Louisa. "It wouldn't say a thing, because it's a horrid, beastly bird and if Bertie were here he would shoot it!" Her voice was getting louder, and Julia thought she had probably forgotten the part about remaining silent. The falcon flapped its wings once, twice, cocking its head to the other side, and Louisa gave a soft whimper and scrambled away to the cover of the reeds. Peter sighed again and ran a hand through his wind-tousled hair. He had absolutely no idea what to do.

"I suppose we'll have to scout out the land," he told Julia. "We can find out if the ship has arrived with the prisoners, and what they're doing with them." Julia nodded, then hesitated as they both looked at Louisa's weeping form.

It was quiet for a long moment.

"We'll help her," Peter said finally. "We can't just stay here." He took his father's compass out of his pocket, flicked it open, studied it for a brief moment, and pointed to the right. "That way," he said. He picked up the satchel of food—what remained of it—and Julia, deciding not to question Peter's sense of direction, went over to the reeds to help Louisa to her feet.

"Come on," she said to her stepsister. "It's time for us to go."

The going was hard—much harder than it had been back in Aedyn. There was no path to speak of, and all they had to go on was Peter's compass. They found themselves crawling over huge boulders and ducking under fallen trees, and it wasn't long before all three of them were covered from head to toe in mud and scratches and bites from the insects that swarmed around them. Louisa's complaints had taken on a desperate, screeching tone that meant she was not far from tears. Julia, who had believed she hated nothing in the world so much as heights, was discovering that in fact she hated the buzzing whine of Khemia's insects a great deal more, and did not spare a thought for her stepsister. And Peter stayed focused on the terrain, moving slowly but always to the east.

As they walked they began to smell something rotten in the air. It grew worse as they continued trudging over the rough terrain, and the children found that they were all holding their breath, taking gasping breaths of stagnant air just when their lungs were ready to burst.

"Oh, it's horrid," cried Louisa at last. "It smells like something rotten and dead."

"It's sulfur," said Peter. "It must be coming from the mine. Here ..." He stopped and took the satchel he'd been carrying off his shoulder, rummaging about in it for a moment before retrieving a bright green woolen scarf. He thrust it at Louisa. "Tie this around your face. It'll be warm, but it'll cut some of the smell." She took it without a word and tied it in a clumsy knot at the back of her head. Julia noticed that she'd managed to tie a great deal of hair into it as well.

The smell grew even more dank and choking as they continued, and the wet heat hung around them like a blanket. Peter, Julia, and Louisa all privately thought that they had never in their lives been quite so miserable. And just as they were thinking it, the situation became a good deal worse.

A fallen tree trunk was lying across their path. There was only a narrow space between the tree and the ground, but the trunk must have been six feet across— too thick for any of them to easily climb over it. Peter was just about to drop down and crawl underneath when the earth opened up in front of him.

There was a sound like screaming as the ground broke away and steam poured out of the fissure. It smelled of something rotten that had been concealed in the earth far too long, and Julia thought—though she did not remember it until later—that she had heard words in the screaming.

Peter had, not for the first time, gone absolutely white with terror. A few more feet, a bit quicker under that fallen tree trunk, and the fissure would have opened right under his feet. He closed his eyes and tried to steady himself, forcing down the wave of nausea that was rising in his stomach. He cleared his throat and stared straight ahead, not wanting to look back at the girls and let them see how frightened he was. He could hear Julia and Louisa's gasping breaths behind him, and he inhaled deeply to settle himself.

"We'll go around that way," Peter said, pretending to look at the compass. He started forward and heard the girls' quiet footsteps behind him. He wanted to run—wanted to get wherever it was they were going before the earth opened up again—but Julia and Louisa might not be able to keep up, and anyway who was to say that the ground was any safer closer to the volcano?

But there were no more earthquakes or fissures, and after a time Peter's face returned to its normal color. They continued east, and after a few miles they found themselves in a clearing at the top of a hill. They looked out over the forest and saw, under a red sky, a great plain laid out before them. And in the center of the plain was the volcano.

It was massive—far greater than it had appeared when they had first seen it from the falcon's back. At its base there was a huge gash in the earth, and even from this distance the children could see hundreds of people swarming around it, all of them bent under heavy loads and the whips of their masters. The wave of nausea returned to Peter's stomach, and he bent over and was violently sick into a patch of bushes.

CHAPTER

8

Julia watched the scene before her, tears swimming in front of her vision. Smoke poured forth from the great scar in the earth, and even from this distance they could hear the groan of machinery. Peter returned from the bushes, wiping the back of his hand across his mouth, and stood beside his sister. And as they watched they heard Louisa behind them.

She was humming again—that same song she always seemed to have stuck in her head—but standing here before the volcano, looking at the task that lay before them, the song seemed different. Haunting, almost. It unnerved Peter almost to the core, and he shivered despite the heat.

"Stop that," he said, and Louisa's humming stopped as quickly as it had begun. "We can't be heard. Come on. Follow me."

The compass wasn't necessary now—they were headed toward the volcano, and there was no mistaking where it was—but Peter still led the way, his father's gift firmly in hand. They walked out of the clearing and down a steep ridge. The going was hard, over the same rocks and thorns that had plagued their steps before, but despite the terrain and the heat and the constant whine of insects there were no complaints. All three of them were intent on getting to the volcano, and getting there quickly.

The smell of sulfur was becoming unbearable. Louisa seemed to be the only one who wasn't badly affected—perhaps because of the makeshift mask Peter had fashioned for her out of his scarf. Julia was almost choking on the stale air, tripping over fallen logs and sharp rocks as she tried to catch her breath. And then she stumbled into Peter's arm, held out as stiff as a suit of armor. She looked up through stinging, red-rimmed eyes to see that they had arrived.

The volcano loomed before them, its mouth yawning open and belching acrid smoke. Miners moved back and forth across the gash in its southern edge, all covered from head to toe in black dust. The men dug and shoveled as the women carted away buckets full of soil to a group of children, who were pawing through the dirt as if searching for something precious. The older children, Julia saw, were moving among the miners with buckets of water, holding dripping ladles up to the lips of the grown-ups. And there was something else— something that was not a man.

There were dozens of these creatures moving among the miners. They were perhaps twice the size of Peter, each one thick and hulking and with arms the size of small trees. Their skin was dark and swarthy, blistered by the sun and by innumerable scars. Peter, who prided himself on never being afraid of anything, felt himself shrinking back in revulsion. The eyes under those massive brows were small and dark, but there was intelligence in their faces. These monsters were not just dumb animals.

Louisa gave a small cry as she saw them. Julia, not stopping to think, grabbed her stepsister's hand in hers and squeezed as tight as she could. Louisa was still, but Julia could feel her shivering as they watched the creatures. They moved to and fro among the workers, and as the children watched, one of them swung its arm back and knocked a man to the ground. He lay still, not moving even after the creature had passed. The work went on around him; no one stopped to help.

Julia shifted her gaze and found herself focusing on a child—a boy, she thought, not much younger than

herself. He was walking along the edge of the workers, close by the clearing, offering his water to the women carrying their loads of dirt. He handed up his ladle to a bedraggled, beaten woman with ragged clothing— more ragged than most. The woman released her load and gratefully accepted the ladle, drinking slowly and deeply. And as she raised her face to drink the last cool drops, Julia gave a little cry.

Peter shot her an accusing glare and put his finger angrily to his lips, but Julia shook her head. "Alyce," she said in a voice that was barely a whisper. "It's Alyce. That woman, over there—no, there." Peter squinted his eyes and peered in the direction indicated.

"Are you sure?" He squinted harder. "It might be. She's so much older …" He shook his head. "I can't tell."

"Who's Alyce?" Louisa had removed the scarf from her face and was trying to look over Peter's shoulder at the woman. Her voice was a good deal louder than a whisper, and Peter shot her a furious glance.

"A friend from before," murmured Julia. "She's not far. I can get her."

"*Get* her? Are you mad? You'll be seen." Peter gave a shake of his head and considered the matter final.

"No one's watching," protested Julia. "Look—she can't be a stone's throw away. The guards are turned away—I can reach her …" And, just like that, she had darted out from behind the cover of the trees, deaf to Peter's hoarsely whispered protests.

The landscape was barren but for a few of the same boulders that had littered their path to the volcano. Julia, keeping a wary eye on the guards, crouched behind the largest one she could find.

"Alyce!" she whispered huskily. *"Alyce!"*

The woman who had drunk from the child's ladle turned, the heavy buckets she had just picked up quivering in her hands. She looked around for the source of the voice, and when she saw where it had come from her eyes opened wider than Julia had ever seen them. Something changed in her face, the burdens of the past weeks fading into relief. Alyce dropped her load and started forward.

Just as she did so, one of the creatures turned and saw that Alyce had stepped out of the line—saw that she had put down her pails. His fist clenched as he changed direction, heading straight for Alyce.

Julia tried without words to warn Alyce of the danger, but the creature's fist caught her before she could react. It was attached to an arm the size of a small tree, and she fell to her knees with a startled cry of pain. The creature moved away with a growl, off to find his next victim, and a guard came up to Alyce, watching her still figure as he coiled a whip around his meaty hand. Julia cowered behind the rock, willing herself to become invisible. The guard was so close she could have reached out and touched his feet. She forced herself to breathe slowly, feeling the gazes of Peter and Louisa on her back.

The guard looked at Alyce for a moment, then reached out his foot and gave her a swift kick in the ribs. "Scum," he muttered, and then turned and was gone.

Alyce wasn't moving. Julia didn't dare to whisper her name again, so she watched and waited, not daring to go out in the open but unwilling to go back to the forest without her. And then she heard footsteps behind her, running quickly and urgently. Peter.

He tapped her on the shoulder and ran out from behind the boulder. He grasped Alyce's motionless body from beneath her shoulders and started dragging her back toward the trees. Julia, suddenly understanding, ran out and took a firm hold of her ankles, and together they hauled her back to safety like a lumpy sack of so many potatoes.

They laid her down once they were about fifty feet into the woods, where they could be certain of not being seen. The blow had knocked the breath from Alyce's body, and her breath came in low, shallow gasps. The left side of her face was smeared with dirt and blood where she had fallen, and Julia wiped at it with the cleanest part of her skirt. It did little good.

"That guard almost saw you!" Louisa was hissing. "The same one who kicked her — he was turning to look just as you got back into the trees!"

"Yes, and if we'd been seen we jolly well would have been beaten — or worse," said Peter. "Just had to go out there, didn't you Julia? Had to see how close you could come to getting us thrown in another dungeon!"

"It's Alyce! We couldn't just leave her out there!" And any further argument was cut off, because Alyce was waking up.

She groaned and lifted herself up to a sitting position. She cringed as she twisted her shoulders, still feeling the blow from the monster, but gave a crooked smile nonetheless. "You've come," she said. "My dear friends. You've grown, Julia. And Peter"—she reached out and took Peter's hand in hers. "You are becoming a man." She smiled, and a faraway look came into her eyes. "We called, and the Lord of Hosts has answered. He has sent you once again." Julia took her hand and squeezed it.

"We've come," she said. "Seems you can't manage without us anymore."

This brought a laugh to Alyce's lips, and then another wince. She put a hand up to her face and looked as if she was trying very hard not to think about the pain. "And it seems you've brought another with you," she said, looking at Louisa.

Louisa, for once, was neither crying nor fainting nor humming, but watching Alyce with her eyes wide, her gaze focused on the blood oozing from her cheek. Peter thought that he had never seen her so transfixed.

"This is Louisa," he said. "Our stepsister. She was …" He paused, giving her a look that might almost be described as puzzled. "She was called here too."

"Welcome, Louisa," said Alyce. "I wish that we could have met under different circumstances, and I could show you all around our fair land. But perhaps that time will come soon."

"Tell us what happened," Julia encouraged. "Tell us what happened to you. Tell us what happened in Aedyn."

Alyce closed her eyes and leaned back against a tree. "It's not a happy story, Julia."

"I didn't think it was. Please."

Alyce nodded. "Not many years after you left," she said, "our people stopped attending the Great Remembrance. They said they were safe, that the Lord of Hosts had saved them from slavery and there was no more danger, no reason to remember such dark times. And soon they could see no reason to remember the Lord of Hosts himself. It was simple: they just forgot, and they thought the good times would last forever."

She stopped and touched her cheek. The blood was beginning to clot. "Go on," prompted Peter.

"We started to hear rumors," Alyce continued. "Rumors of another power. And the people said that this power was stronger than anything we had ever known—that they had been right to forget the Lord of Hosts. So when the soldiers from Khemia came, they prayed to the wrong god. They prayed to the one who couldn't save them.

"The soldiers came in waves. They took the first prisoners about a year ago. Our king had disbanded the army just after the dark lords fell—it was thought that we didn't need the protection because there was no longer any threat. And the king would not fight against the Khemians, because he was certain—so, so certain—that the god they worshipped was the true power in our world.

"So the soldiers came back, and there was still no one to fight. Oh, some tried. My husband, Lukas, tried to organize the men, but it was already too late. They took a few of us at a time—never enough of us to cause trouble on the journey over. And when we arrived at this cursed land we found the mines."

She shrugged, looking all but hopeless.

"What are you all mining for?" asked Peter.

"I don't know," Alyce replied. "None of us do. We think it must be something to do with their god—whatever power it is that's living in the earth."

"Power?" asked Peter. "What power?"

It was a moment before Alyce answered, and when she did her voice was very soft. The three children had to lean in to catch her next words.

"There's something else here," she was saying. "Something else inside the earth. I don't know if it's a god or a devil, but there's something inside that volcano. And it wants to get out."

A shiver went through the children.

"Wants to get out?" repeated Peter after a moment.

"There was an earthquake," said Julia. "And back in the woods, when we were coming here—something happened. The earth seemed to open up and—and it sounded like someone screaming." Julia had been hesitant to speak, afraid that she would sound foolish, but she saw that Alyce was nodding.

"We've seen it too," she said. "It's been happening more and more. Earthquakes, the earth falling away from under our feet—something is moving under the earth. The volcano has been smoking more and more since we came. The evil wants to get out into the world, and the Khemians' mine is only speeding it on its way."

"But what is it they're looking for?" insisted Peter.

"Something secret," said Alyce. "Something that has been buried for many years. We've been told no more than that. If we find anything unusual, anything at all, we're to take it to the guards."

"Have you found anything yet?" asked Louisa.

"Rocks," Alyce said with a grimace. "Lots and lots of rocks. We've been at it for months, and the guards are starting to become impatient. Their Captain especially."

"How do we find him?" asked Peter.

Julia shot him a glance. "What are you intending to do?" she asked.

"I don't know yet, but it might be good to know who our enemy is."

"The Captain doesn't come down here much," said Alyce. "You'll most likely find him in his tent. It's back up there, at the top of the ridge." She pointed to a not-too-distant spot. "His name is Ceres, and you'll recognize him by the talisman he always wears—a great green stone, with the shape of a star cut out of it. But be careful—he's a dangerous man, and he does

not have a great deal of patience. It is he who controls
the Gul'nog."

"The ... who?"

"Those creatures." Alyce twisted her shoulders,
trying to squeeze the ache out of them. "It's said that
they were men once—men twisted into monsters by
that dark power. Praise the Lord of Hosts that you've
come. You'll find a way to defeat this power and take us
back to Aedyn—I know it."

At these words Peter's back straightened and a
small smile grew on his lips. He remembered the old en-
ergy that had come to him back in Aedyn—the power
he'd felt with a bow in his hands, the string taut against
his fingers, the arrow pointed straight and true. Let his
father say now that he wasn't a man!

After a moment, Peter realized that Alyce was
addressing him. "Remember, Peter, that Ceres and his
Gul'nog are not your greatest enemies here. Your enemy
is the people, and their anger against the Lord of Hosts.
It is they who must be changed before you can work
your good in Khemia."

Peter wanted to protest, Julia could tell—he
wanted an enemy that was easier to face. But he simply
nodded, and Alyce smiled.

"For my part, I will do everything I can to help
you. I will tell the people that you have returned." She
stood. "I have to get back before I'm missed."

"Don't go!" Louisa cried. "Stay here with us—don't go out there to be hurt again!"

"I have to," Alyce said simply. "My son is out there. I won't leave him." She embraced each of them in turn. "You are most welcome here," she said. "I thank the Lord of Hosts that his Deliverers have returned." She smiled and slipped out from between the trees, back out to the mine.

CHAPTER

9

Peter, Julia, and Louisa watched as Alyce returned to the mine, straining to pick up her buckets full of dirt and returning to the line with the other women. "She's already been through so much," murmured Julia. "It's wrong that she should have to endure this as well."

"Of course it is," said Peter, putting a hand on her arm. "And that's why we're here—to make sure that she and the others will never have to endure it again. You all right? And you, Louisa? Ready to keep walking?"

"But where are we going?" Louisa asked. "I thought we were looking for the volcano. And here we are. What do we do next?"

"We're going to find the captain of the guard, of course," said Peter. "There's nothing we can do here. Not just yet. We can't talk to the people when the guards are watching. There will be time enough for that later on." He eyed the ridge that Alyce had pointed out. "It's not far … but perhaps we should have a bit of that cheese and sausage first."

The three children dug into the contents of the satchel. Peter warned them only to drink the water they needed, and to save as much as they could, but between them they emptied one of the skins. Peter congratulated himself on having had the foresight to gather food from the castle, and Julia, much as she hated to let Peter be right, had to admit that it was a very lucky thing indeed. And once they had eaten their fill, they packed away the remaining things and started, once more, on their trip through the woods.

Peter had been right: the ridge with the guards' tents wasn't far away, but they had to keep quiet and move stealthily, and that is not a particularly easy thing to do when one is tired and has just had a good meal. Through the trees they could see a path leading from the volcano up to the ridge. They moved parallel to it, always keeping it in sight. Each of them would have liked very much to walk on it, as there weren't nearly as many boulders to slow their progress or branches to slap back in their faces, but they had no idea how often the path was used and knew they couldn't risk being seen.

As they walked Louisa began to hum once again. Each time Peter and Julia heard it the melody seemed more distinct, more haunting, lingering in their ears long after she'd ceased. Julia couldn't quite describe what the song did to her, but she felt deep in her bones that the music must mean something.

"What's that song, Louisa?" she asked. "The one you're always humming—what is it?"

"I don't know," said Louisa, surprised. "It's something I've always known." Julia fell quiet and Louisa resumed her song, and on they walked.

It wasn't long before the path beside them opened up into a great clearing in which stood a grouping of makeshift shelters. Jagged stumps of trees dotted the space between the shelters. To call them tents would be generous, thought Julia, for they were constructed of little but a large piece of cloth slung over a few poles. They could hear noises from within—a few hacking coughs and creaking groans. "Those must be the ones who are too sick to work," said Louisa, and Peter and Julia nodded.

As they watched a bedraggled figure emerged from one of the tents. His clothes were hanging off his gaunt frame, and his face had taken on a sickly shade of green. He stumbled as he walked, not quite able to keep his balance. A hacking cough overtook him, coming from deep within his lungs, as he staggered to another one of the tents.

Peter turned his face from the sick man and looked around the clearing. "Over there," he said, pointing up a hill to the far side, away from the shelters. "That must be where the guards are." Even from this distance they could see that the tents were almost luxurious by comparison—vaulted ceilings and doors, and certainly capable of keeping their occupants safe from any bad weather. "Follow me," Peter said, and he began to creep along behind the prisoners' tents. Julia followed.

"No," said Louisa.

Peter turned and looked at her. "What?"

"I'm not going. I'm staying here with the sick people."

"You can't stay here," Peter said bluntly. "Anyone might see you. You've got to stay with us."

"I was called here just as much as you, Mr. Deliverer," she said, her hands planted firmly on her hips. "You two go on and spy on the guards. I'm going to stay and see to the sick people here. They need help and I can give it to them. I'll tell them all about your Lord of Hosts, just as you would do. I can *help.*" She stamped her foot on the last word.

Peter did not know what to do. On the one hand it might be quite helpful to have Louisa stay and minister to the sick—it would be a start on what he believed was the work they were meant to do here. And yet he wasn't entirely sure that she could be trusted not to make a mess of things. He stammered, his mouth hanging open as he debated.

Julia reached out and put a hand on Peter's arm. "That's fine, Louisa," she said. "That's exactly as it should be. Be careful, and get out and hide in the trees if anything goes wrong. Remember, you can't be seen by any of the Khemians."

Peter was still stammering. "I'll be fine, Peter," said Louisa. "Come find me when you get back, all right?"

He nodded. "*Do* be careful," he cautioned. "And see if you can get any information on the mines."

"I will," she said, and ducked into one of the shelters. Peter looked after her for a moment, and then Julia pulled him away.

"She'll be fine," she said as they walked uphill to the guards' tents. "She hasn't fainted for—oh, it must have been hours now. A marked improvement, really."

"I don't know if she can be trusted," Peter replied stiffly. "The only side she's on is her own."

"Do you really think so?" asked Julia. "She seems different lately—not so horrid as she was back home. Did you see how she was watching Alyce? It was—well, it was almost as if she cared. And wanting to stay with the sick people, wanting to help them … something must be changing her." She smiled, then said, half to herself, "Perhaps the Lord of Hosts is at work, even in this pit of a place."

And then Peter shushed her, because they were approaching the tent of the captain of the guards. It could only have been his tent: it was the finest in the clearing, with embroidered fabric swinging over the entrance and room for twenty men to stand inside. It looked as if there were separate rooms, all with tables and chairs and ornately woven rugs.

The two children hid themselves near the back of the tent, just a few steps away from the woods. They wouldn't be seen by any guards unless someone was looking for them, but they could hear perfectly every word spoken inside.

"I grow tired of waiting," a voice was saying. "Seven months it has been — seven months! And in that time the prisoners have turned up nothing. Nothing but a few rocks and worms." The children heard another man clearing his throat.

"Sir, if I may ... the area we've been searching is large indeed, and it may not be realistic to expect ..." He was interrupted by the sound of a fist crashing down on the table.

"I *expect* to be obeyed. I *expect* results. Look here," said the first voice. Peter and Julia could hear the shuffling of papers inside the tent. "Here, right at the top. The prophecy. You see, gentlemen? You see why this is of the most extreme importance?"

"I didn't say it wasn't important, Captain. I meant that the map is not specific, and it could be years before we uncover …" The voice went silent and was replaced by a sort of heavy breathing.

"Years?" said the first voice quietly. "Look around you. The smell. The quakes in the earth. The fissures. We do not have years; we have days. If we do not find the second half before that time we are all doomed." There was a long pause, and more of the heavy breathing. "Doomed, gentlemen. I suggest you try harder."

"The prisoners are digging as fast as they can," put in a third voice timidly.

"Then you'll have to dig yourself!" The Captain's quiet voice was gone, and Peter thought with a shudder that Captain Ceres sounded exactly like his father when he was angry. They heard the sound of chairs scraping and footsteps over hard ground. The guards were leaving.

Julia moved from the tent to creep back to the trees, but Peter stuck out an arm in front of her. "Listen," he said. A bottle was being opened, and some liquid was being poured into a glass. Julia could hear the splashing. "Wait," Peter mouthed. "Maybe he'll sleep."

They waited as the Captain downed his drink, then poured himself another, then another. Their limbs

were getting stiff as they crouched against the tent, but
they dared not move or make a noise. And then, finally,
after what felt like hours later, came the sound of a glass
falling and hitting the floor. It was followed by a series of
thunderous snores, and Peter grinned at his sister. "Now,"
he said.

They stood and took a moment to ease their aching legs and knees, then went slowly around to the front
of the tent. Julia lifted one of the heavy tent flaps and
peered inside. Ceres, the captain of the guard, lay back in
a chair behind his desk, one hand folded over his ample
stomach and the other hovering over the glass that had
fallen to the floor. Before him was a desk strewn with a
mess of papers. But Julia's gaze was drawn to the Captain's
chest. There was a large talisman laying there, attached to
a cord that went around his neck. The talisman had six
long sides, and out of the center had been cut the shape
of a star. Julia had the most curious feeling that she'd seen
it before ... but it looked wrong, somehow.

Peter was behind her, hissing at her to move so
he could get inside and have a look at the papers. Julia
came to her senses and was about to step aside when the
earth began to shake.

It was worse—much worse—than any earthquake they'd felt so far on the island. The ground
seemed to roar as it shuddered, collapsing the tents and
knocking Peter and Julia from their feet. Together they

tumbled down the hill, grabbing at anything they could
hold onto, trying not to yell as the rocks and branches on
the ground tore their clothes and scratched their skin.
And finally, mercifully, the earthquake ended almost
as quickly as it had begun. And Peter and Julia found
themselves lying at the feet of a particularly nasty-look-
ing guard.

He released the tree he had been grabbing onto
for support and scowled at the children. "Thought we'd
get off work, did we?" he sneered, and Julia and Peter
recognized him as the third voice they'd heard back in

the tent. "Maybe it's the sting of my whip you need to teach you." Peter shook his head, his lips white.

"N ... no sir," he stammered. Julia was absolutely silent, her eyes riveted on that whip.

"On your feet, you scum!" They scrambled up, and Peter saw that with the dark dust on their clothes they looked the same as any other prisoner. "March!"

Peter looked down and realized that they were standing on the path they'd seen from the forest—the path that led to the mine. The guard slapped the handle of his whip against their backs and repeated his command, and they started walking.

The path curved around the prisoners' tents, and Julia stole a glance up at them. They had all collapsed in the earthquake, and a few bedraggled figures were just emerging from the rubble of cloth and sticks. A young woman that she hardly recognized as her stepsister was moving among them, helping them out from the wreckage of their shelter and letting them lean on her shoulder. As she worked Julia heard her singing that familiar, haunting melody. But this time the song had words.

Peter had noticed Louisa as well. He stared up at her, mouth agape, forgetting entirely that he was supposed to be walking, forgetting that there was a guard with a vicious-looking whip behind him. He didn't remember the whip until its sting came cracking down across his back.

CHAPTER

10

Peter's knees buckled under the sting of the whip, and the next thing he knew his face was pressed into the rocky sand of the road. His back felt as if it had been slashed in two, and the pain took his breath away.

He gasped for air, trying not to cry out, and felt Julia's hands on his shoulders. "Peter," she was saying. "Peter, get up. You have to get up. Let me help you ..."

She was interrupted by the guard, who gave a swift kick to Peter's side as he growled for him to rise. "Up, scum," he snarled. "Thought you'd take your time, did you? Thought you'd take a nice stroll back to the mine? On your feet, boy."

Peter planted his hands on either side of his shoulders and pushed himself up. The stinging spread like a fire across his arms, bringing another gasp of pain to his lips. Julia had her arms around him and lifted him to his feet, stumbling under his weight.

"Come on," she whispered. "Come on. It's not bad. You have to keep walking." Peter grunted and took one step, then another, trying to put his mind to anything but the agony in his side and across his shoulders.

The road to the mine felt ten times as long as it had before. Every shuddering breath was another stab where the guard had kicked him, and the air Peter drew into his lungs seemed even more foul than it had before.

The smell of sulfur grew stronger as they approached the mines once again. Coming to the end of the path, the guard gave both Peter and Julia a non-too-gentle shove in the direction of the cistern, where the older children were filling their water buckets.

"To work," he said. "You won't be trying to escape again, and if you do you can be sure that the Gul'nog will make you regret it. I'll be watching," he promised.

Peter and Julia bent to pick up buckets that were standing ready by the cistern, dipping them into the stagnant pool. Julia, for her part, could hardly believe how heavy a full pail of water could be, but she looked at Peter and saw that he was hefting the rope handle onto his shoulder. She could see by the way he was gritting his teeth that it was hurting him. A year ago he wouldn't have been able to do it, she thought. The pain and the weariness would have been too much for him. But when it came to that, a year ago she would have been just as helpless. Julia slung the ropes over her shoulders and, along with her brother, joined the masses of weary prisoners.

The two children moved among the captive people of Aedyn, lifting ladles full of water to cracked and thirsty lips. With each dipper of water Peter and Julia whispered the good news they brought with them. "The Deliverers have returned. The Lord of Hosts is calling you back. Cry out to him—he is already answering." At one point Julia thought she saw Alyce, perhaps whispering the same words as she carried her load of earth to the groups of younger children, but she was too far away to be certain. And slowly, slowly, but ever so certainly, the rumor began to spread.

It was a long, horrible afternoon. The sun beat down upon the baking ground, scorching the earth and all who worked on it. Peter, who had privately fancied that he could stand just about anything, found himself wilting under the unrelenting heat, the welts on his back stinging anew as the ropes from the water bucket cut into the sores. After only an hour his dust-stained clothes had been soaked through with sweat, and he indulged himself in a sip from his own water bucket. The day pressed on into evening, and as the light began to fade Peter could hardly imagine that just last night he had been flying over the sea on the back of a falcon, the wind in his hair and the stars in his eyes.

He thought that the guards might have worked their prisoners on through the night, but Captain Ceres himself must have realized the foolishness of searching for a hidden object when no one could see two steps in front of him. One of the guards blew a horn, and all around him people laid down their shovels and pails and joined a long line following the road up to the tents. Peter walked slowly, scanning all the faces for some sign of Julia. But every face looked the same in the fading light.

Finally he spotted her. He never would have recognized her but for her fair hair—nearly everyone in Aedyn and Khemia was dark. Her hair shone even under the dust and sweat of the day, and he hurried to catch up with her.

"Found you," he said into her ear, and she turned to give him a tired grin.

"Are you all right?" she asked, glancing at the tatters of his shirt.

Peter nodded curtly. "I'm fine," he said.

Julia thought that probably he was lying, and reached down to squeeze his hand. "The people are listening, Peter!" she said after a moment, her voice quiet so as not to attract attention. "Well ... some. Not all. Some of them are so angry. They say that if the Lord of Hosts existed he would never abandon his people. But the others—they remember what it was like before, and they're listening." Her eyes were bright and hopeful, and Peter wondered if she ever got discouraged.

"We'll take them back home," he said, and squeezed the hand that he still held. "Now we just need to find Louisa."

There were groans of frustration as the prisoners approached the ridge and found that their shelters had all fallen down in the earthquake. There is perhaps nothing quite so miserable as returning home at the end of a day, eager to lay down your head and rest your eyes, and discovering that there is a great deal of work left to be done. But in the swiftly fading light they set to repairing the tents, for who else would help them?

Peter and Julia held tight to each other's hands in the crowd, trying to stay together. And they found Louisa right where they had left her: standing with the sick prisoners, singing softly to them as the repairs went on around them.

> The two come together; the two become one
> With union comes power, control over all
> Flooded by light, the shadow outdone,
> The Host shall return; the darkness shall fall.

It was the same song they had heard her singing earlier, when they were being marched to the mine. Neither of them knew what the words meant, and wondered how Louisa had come to know them. It wasn't like any song they'd ever heard at home.

Peter, not distracted by the music, called out Louisa's name. She looked up and smiled, seeming relieved to see them. She flipped her stringy braids over her shoulders and ran over.

"Where have you *been?*" she asked. "You left ages ago, and I thought you might be in some kind of trouble."

"No trouble," said Peter, holding his shoulders stiffly. "We were taken to the mine by a guard after the earthquake."

"Were you all right?" asked Julia eagerly. "In the earthquake, I mean?"

Louisa nodded. "There wasn't much to fall down on us." Peter was impressed in spite of himself. Only a day ago she would have had hysterics and fainted. The air of this place must be changing her.

"Come on," he said. "There won't be room for us to sleep here with the prisoners, and I won't take up a bed that ought to go to someone who needs it more. We'll camp out in the forest tonight."

None of the three was particularly excited at this prospect, but Louisa gathered up a few blankets and they slipped out from the camp to the cover of the trees.

They found a spot not far from the prisoners' camp and cleared out the dead leaves and rocks before they lay down. They covered themselves in the thread-bare blankets Louisa had brought along. They weren't much to keep them warm, but they were certainly better than nothing.

Perhaps you have, at some time in your life, spent a night camping outdoors. Perhaps you had a tent and a fire starter and a good fluffy pillow and plenty of blankets. You might have been kept awake by all of the unusual night sounds of the outdoors but you managed to get a very decent night's sleep overall.

Peter, Julia, and Louisa did not have such a good sleep. It was rotten and uncomfortable. They were all three badly in need of a bath and a good meal, for it is nearly impossible to sleep when one's stomach is growling. Twigs and sharp rocks poked into their backs, and the night air grew distinctly chilly. They huddled close together and pulled the blankets tight around them, but still they couldn't get properly comfortable.

At some point during the night—it must have been well after midnight, but of course none of them could be sure—Peter rolled over onto his side and stood up. Julia grabbed at his leg.

"Where do you think you're going?" she asked urgently.

"I'm going back to the Captain's tent," he replied. "I just want to get another look at those papers that were on his desk. Whatever those guards were talking about sounded important."

"Don't go, Peter," said Julia. "It's too dangerous. You'll be caught."

"I'll be careful," he promised. "Stay here. I'll be back before you know it." And he slipped away between the trees.

He moved around the outside edge of the camp, thankful for the light of the full moon that night. He crept behind the makeshift shelters until he found himself back at the Captain's tent. Those same thunderous snores were coming from deep within, and Peter lifted up one of the tent flaps and stepped inside.

The Captain wasn't there, but he could hear him off in another section of the tent. Two guards lay on cots stretched out in front of the desk, but both of them appeared to be sleeping soundly. Peter watched them for a moment, standing still in the doorway with his hand holding up the flap, but once he was satisfied that neither of them would wake, he stepped inside.

On the desk was the same mess of papers that had been there earlier in the day. He stepped gingerly over to the desk and looked at the papers that lay on top. Lists of names, longer lists of numbers, plans for some sort of building. And then a larger paper, the width of his arm, yellowed and wrinkled with age, the sides curling up on each other as if they were accustomed to being rolled up. Peter slid it out from underneath the others and squinted his eyes, trying to make out the writing on it, but it was too detailed to read in the half-light of the candles in the tent. He rolled it up, being careful not to let the paper crackle, and turned to leave the tent.

But just as he was going the end of the rolled-up parchment smacked against a glass inkpot that had been sitting on the desk. It knocked the pot with enough force that it fell on its side and then, before Peter could reach out to stop it, rolled off the desk and clattered to the floor. It shattered at once, and dark liquid splashed all over the broken pieces of glass. Both guards woke and leapt to their feet.

CHAPTER

11

It took Peter an instant to react. He stared in horror at the guards, and then, just as one reached out to grab him, he bolted out the door and fled behind the Captain's tent into the dark woods. He ran and ran, ran for all he was worth, but more than once he felt the brush of hard fingertips against his shoulder blade. Two sets of heavy footsteps matched his every step, never seeming to tire.

Peter couldn't see much in front of him—just the dark outlines of trees and rocks in his path. He ducked over and under branches, desperately sucking air into his lungs as he forced his tired limbs forward. And then, all of a sudden, the ground seemed to fall out from under his feet. He stumbled clumsily down a steep ravine, his feet tripping over themselves and the mess of branches on the forest floor. He grappled to find his footing, and, to his relief, heard the guards trying to do the same. Their stumbling bought him another few moments. At last he found the bottom of the ravine and tripped into a few inches of water.

The river was shallow but swift. He splashed straight through to the opposite bank, listening for the splash of the guards as they too fell into the river. They were a second behind him, but only a second. Reaching the bank, Peter clambered up the side of the ravine, using his hands and feet to grab at anything that would hold him. The guards were falling further behind now: Peter was slight and athletic, and despite their strength the guards' weight was slowing them down as they climbed. Some sixth sense in Peter understood this, and knowing that they weren't directly on his heels he swerved sharply to the left.

Even through the dark of the night he could see the shape of a huge tree coming up in front of him—the trunk so large it would take four men to circle it. Peter ducked to its opposite side and leaned back against it, holding in his breath and trying not to pant. He closed his eyes tight, squeezed his hand around the roll of parchment, and breathed a silent prayer to the Lord of Hosts that he would not be seen.

The guards had seen him run to the side and had followed, but they soon became disoriented. Ten yards beyond the tree where Peter was hiding they stopped, confused.

"Where did he go?" one asked the other. "We just had him—he was right here."

"Search the trees," the other replied. "He's got to be hiding somewhere near here." In the half-light of the moon that filtered through the trees Peter could see him put his fingers to his lips, and as he waited the guard let out a shrill whistle.

The sound of it pierced the air, and Peter knew that whatever it signaled would not be kind to him. He watched and waited, listening hard into the darkness.

As he waited the guards split up and began to comb the area. Peter slowly and cautiously edged his way around to the other side of the tree, still holding his breath. He waited there for what seemed an eternity but could only have been a few minutes, and gradually realized that the guards had moved on, searching deeper into the woods. He breathed a deep sigh of utter relief and turned back the way he had come ...

... Only to be confronted by the hulking form of a Gul'nog.

It towered over him, its lips curled into a snarl over rotting teeth and its meaty arms poised to kill. Each arm ended in a fist the size of Peter's head. Peter stood still, not moving, not breathing, clutching the scroll of paper that was crinkled tight in his hand. And then, almost without thinking, he turned on his heel and sprinted off between the trees.

Peter could feel the hot breath of the Gul'nog on his back, hear the thunderous weight of its feet crashing toward him through the underbrush. Peter ducked under low-hanging branches and leaped over bushes, ducking this way and that between the trees, trying with all his might to stay ahead of the monster. He zigzagged through the woods, turning abruptly to the left or the right to evade the Gul'nog's claws. His lungs were on fire but he forced himself forward, forced himself to stay those few steps ahead. There was no time for thought, no time for planning. Only one word was left in Peter's mind: *run*.

He ran for what felt like miles, the Gul'nog always close behind. The creature never seemed to tire, swatting aside tree limbs as if they had been nothing more than a tiresome insect. Peter could only be thankful that he was alone—that he didn't have to wait for the girls to keep up ...

The girls. Julia and Louisa. He was leading the Gul'nog straight toward them!

Peter spun to the right and sprinted away. There was no path to follow and some corner of Peter's mind told him that in a few moments he would be hopelessly lost, but still he kept on, steering the Gul'nog away from the place where Julia and Louisa were camped.

And then, just as Peter felt that his lungs were about to burst, he saw his escape.

Up ahead a sheer cliff towered over them. The moonlight illuminated its craggy face—the spiny outcroppings, the caves cloaked in shadows, the—

The cave. Peter could see one, just ahead. It was small, maybe just large enough for him to stand up in, and hidden just at the foot of the cliff. If he could only reach it before the Gul'nog saw it ...

Peter sprinted forward, gaining a stride's worth of ground on the monster. They came up to the cliff and Peter ducked down into the cave's opening, looking back just in time to see the Gul'nog running past.

Peter watched as the creature slowed, then came to a stop as it realized that it had lost its prey. It raised its face to the air and breathed in long and deep, trying to smell him out. Peter shrank back into the recesses of the cave, trying to slow his gasping breaths, certain that the monster would be able to hear the pounding of his heart. But as he watched the Gul'nog started forward once more, heading off into the trees.

Peter collapsed against the cave wall and buried his face in his knees, trying not to think of what the Gul'nog might have done to him had it caught him. And then, after a long moment, Peter looked down at the scroll that was still clutched tightly in his sweaty hand.

He unrolled the long piece of parchment on the floor of the cave, squinting down at the lines of ink that made this paper so important to the Khemians. They'd spoken of some sort of prophecy—there, at the top, was that some sort of writing? But the shadows of the cave made it impossible to see: moonlight could not penetrate here. So Peter hurriedly rolled the parchment back up, stuck the roll in his belt, and sat back to wait.

He should have been tired. He hadn't had a full night's rest since Christmas Eve, after all. But Peter couldn't shut his eyes. There was too much to wonder about, too many strange new noises to listen to, and too many questions to ponder. So he stayed wide awake, looking out into the dark forest and breathing that stagnant air, waiting until he could be quite sure that the guards and the Gul'nog had gone back to their camp.

When he was certain that he was safe, Peter crept out of the cave on his hands and knees, looking all around to be certain that nothing sinister was waiting for him. Seeing nothing but long shadows, he rose to his feet and began the long journey back to the camp.

He had become disoriented in the long flight from the Gul'nog, and he might never have found his bearings in the dark had it not been for the volcano. Looking up through the trees, looking for anything familiar, Peter could see the giant plume of smoke, punctuated by bright flashes of lightning, rising to the sky.

Noting the direction of the volcano, Peter put a hand into his pocket and took out his father's compass. He flipped open the top, realizing as he did so that it was still too dark to see. Finding a patch of moonlight between the trees he squinted at the tiny dial. West, he decided. He would have to head west.

He crept along, keeping to the shadows and trying to keep as silent as he possibly could. He trod slowly when he reached the brook, barely lifting his feet above the water and trying not to splash. He climbed back up the sloping side of the ravine and, after a long walk through the trees during which he lost his way not once but twice, found himself back at the camp.

From there it was simple to find his way back to Julia and Louisa, and found his sister sitting upright with her back against a tree as she waited for him, her eyes wide as she tried to see into the darkness. Louisa, it seemed, had finally been able to get to sleep.

"I thought you'd left us," Julia said simply. "Are you ... what happened?"

"The guards woke up," said Peter. "They chased me, and then they called one of those Gul'nog creatures, and ... well, I had to run."

"Did they follow you?" Her voice was urgent, frightened. Peter shook his head.

"Not this far. I got away." He paused and grinned. "And I got something else." He held out the roll of parchment, wrinkled and sweaty where he'd been grasping it.

Peter rolled out the paper on the ground, and he and Julia both knelt over it. The dawn had just begun to touch the sky after the endless night, and there was just enough light for them to make out what tales the parchment told. It was a map—a map of the whole world. Khemia, its volcano drawn in detail, was at the center of the map, and Aedyn lay near it, marked by its citadel and the King's Garden. But there were other islands too—more than a score of them. There was Melita,

with its great cliffs, and there was Tunbridge, with its acres of vineyards.

"I had no idea their world was this big," murmured Julia.

"Neither did I," said Peter. "It's a whole world—and maybe a whole universe beyond it. Look here—there's something written on the volcano."

They both strained to see what it could be but the light wasn't strong enough, and they resolved to wait until the morning. And then, just as Peter was about to roll up the parchment, Julia pointed to some words at the top.

"Wait. This here—these words. What does it say? The script is so old-fashioned; I can't quite make it out."

Peter leaned forward. The letters were slanted and highly designed, like something out of a Bible from hundreds of years ago. He squinted his eyes and peered a bit closer.

"The two come ... something. The two ... something one. With something comes power, control something ... something."

"Well, that's tremendously helpful," said Julia with a sound that might have been a snort had she not been trying to keep quiet. "Here, let me try." She leaned over the parchment, tilting her head to let what little light there was fall on the words. "The two come ... something."

"Together!" cried Peter. "You see? That right there—that's a *g*."

"That's a *g*?" Julia seemed skeptical.

"Yes, and here"—Peter pointed as he read. "'The two come together; the two ... become one. With—what's that, a *u*?—union! With union comes power, control over all.'" He leaned back and rubbed his hands together, obviously quite pleased with himself. "You see, my dear sister? Nothing to it!"

Julia's brow was furrowed.

"What's wrong?" Peter asked.

"That's the song Louisa was singing when we got back from the mine. Part of it, anyway. How would she have known those words?"

"It can't be the same words." Peter sat back and considered for a moment, then shook his head. "You must be mistaken."

Peter knew perfectly well that Julia had a stubborn streak, and he should have known better than to awaken it. Her back stiffened and her eyes squinted as she glared at him.

"I am *not* mistaken, Peter Grant. She's been humming that song ever since we got to Aedyn, and I heard her singing the words when that horrid guard was marching us to the volcano yesterday afternoon. You heard it yourself—you stopped, and then he whipped you. I *know* that was part of it—that bit about unity and power and control. I'm certain of it."

Peter looked over at Louisa. She was sleeping peacefully, her hands curled up under her head in place of a pillow and the threadbare blanket hunched up around her shoulders.

"What does *she* have to do with this place?" he asked, bewildered.

"She can't have been here before. No one but us has been here," said Julia.

There was a long moment as they watched their stepsister sleep. Finally, Peter reached out and rolled up the long piece of parchment. "We'll ask her about it in the morning," he said. "Look—morning's not far off. Try to catch a few minutes' sleep before then."

He tucked the roll under the crook of his arm and lay down against a tree. Julia gave an unsatisfied *harrumph!* and did the same. But the thoughts that occupied her mind that night, in the minutes before she fell into an exhausted sleep, were not of Louisa and the song. They were of the talisman that had lain against the Captain's chest. She *knew* she had seen it somewhere before.

CHAPTER

12

Julia woke first, not quite an hour later. It had been a troubled evening, and her eyes were red-rimmed and weary. She poked Peter and Louisa awake and peered out from the trees toward the camp. None of the prisoners were awake yet—or at least she didn't see any people moving about.

"Good morning," Louisa mumbled, rubbing a hand across her eyes. She stood up and stretched her arms up above her head, and as she did she began to sing that same haunting melody that had become so familiar.

"Stop singing that!" demanded Peter. Louisa looked up in surprise.

"Why?"

"Because it's a horrid, awful song. Look at this!" Peter unrolled the scroll of paper that had been tucked under his arm while he slept. "Here—right here. This is what you were singing."

Louisa's gray eyes went wide as she looked at the writing along the top of the parchment. "I didn't know," she said. "It's just something that's been in my head for—for ages. Just a melody I picked up somewhere."

"But there was more to what you were singing," said Julia. "More than just these two lines."

"'Flooded by light, the shadow outdone, the Host shall return; the darkness shall fall,'" Louisa recited. All three of the children looked back at the words that crawled along the top of the parchment.

"Why don't they have all of it written out?" asked Peter. "Why only the first two lines?"

"Maybe they don't know the rest of it," said Louisa with a shrug. "Here, what's this?" She pointed to a spot underneath the drawing of the volcano on Khemia. It was an elongated star with six points, and beside it had been scrawled in an unsteady hand, quite different from the writing at the top of the map, *The two come together.*

Julia couldn't take her eyes off it.

"It's like the talisman the Captain was wearing," she said. "Don't you remember, Peter? It had six sides, and there was a space cut out in the middle that would fit a star like this."

Peter shook his head. "I didn't notice any talisman."

"He was wearing one; I'm sure of it. Alyce told us about it, remember? And you know what else she was saying. The prisoners are digging for something. What if this star is what they're searching for? It it's the right size it would fit inside the Captain's talisman, and then—well …" She pointed again to the writing. "'With union comes power; control over all.' They'll have control over …" She paused, uncertain how to continue.

"Over that power in the earth," said Louisa. Peter and Julia shot her surprised glances, but she continued. "Isn't that right? That woman at the mine was saying there's something in the ground that wants to come out, and maybe with this"—she pointed again to the drawing of the star—"maybe if the Khemians have this they can control that power."

"But you're forgetting the next two lines," said Peter. "What does the rest of the rhyme mean? The Host shall return, right?" said Peter. "So what happens when you put the two halves together?"

But before any of them could speak again a long, low horn sounded, and in a moment the camp was abuzz with the sounds of prisoners rising from their beds and guards urging them along, none too gently. Peter rolled up the parchment and, with a quick glance around, found a tree that had been burned and hollowed out. He stuck the rolled-up paper down into the trunk and, satisfied, turned back to the girls.

"We'll keep it safe there," he said. "We'd best go with the prisoners back to the mine. At least we can be of some good there."

But something was happening in the camp. The guards were moving among the prisoners, scattering them with a show of their whips. The guards were all yelling at once, but the three children were too far away to hear what they were saying.

"Come on," said Peter, and they all crept forward, keeping low to the ground and trying not to make any sounds.

"Something was stolen from us last night!" one of the guards was crying. His whip was unfurled, and he flicked it menacingly as he spoke. "The thief will come forward at once! The thief must show himself!"

Julia's face went white. She looked over and saw that Peter's had gone even paler.

"What is it?" said Louisa. "You're the thief? You stole that map last night?"

"Of course it's me," Peter said.

"Well, you'll just have to give it back," said Louisa firmly, and both Peter and Julia recognized the sing-song voice that she had always used back at home when she wanted to be particularly vile. "We've had a good look at it and we don't need it anymore, and if you don't give it back they'll just start hurting someone else."

"I won't do that," Peter hissed through his teeth. "If they want it that badly there must be some reason. We keep it hidden here. We'll go back to the mine and just … do our best to keep our heads down."

It was clear that the discussion was over. Peter stood and made ready to dash out from the forest into the camp, but Julia grabbed at his arm.

"Wait a moment," she said. "Before we go out there we ought to ask the Lord of Hosts for his protection. We won't be able to turn the people back to him unless we know he's fighting on our side, will we?"

She reached out for Peter and Louisa's hands, feeling a bit foolish. They all stood together in a circle and closed their eyes as Julia spoke.

"Lord of Hosts, today we … we ask you to be with us. Give us strength for the task we are about to complete. Show us how to reach the hearts of your people, and show us the way to take them back home." She stopped and lifted her head, smiling at Peter and Louisa. They squeezed one another's hands tight, not yet willing to let go. And as they stood there a wind moved through the trees, the freshest breeze they'd felt or breathed since they'd come to Khemia on the back of the falcon. They all breathed it deeply into their lungs, wanting it to linger and blow away all the evil and wickedness of this place.

"Come on," said Peter, smiling at the two girls. "It's time for us to go." They went once again to the edge of the woods, and breathed a sigh of relief to find that the guards had moved on. They wouldn't be seen coming out from the trees.

They joined the line of prisoners who were marching—shuffling, really—down the rocky path to the volcano. Louisa was humming softly to herself as they went, and Peter remarked privately to Julia that she was getting downright batty about that song.

"At least she's not singing it," replied Julia in a whisper. "Imagine if one of those guards heard her singing, and they realized she knew the other half of their poem or prophecy or whatever it is."

"That's true," Peter acknowledged, and they walked the rest of the way in silence.

It was just a few minutes later that they reached the volcano. Julia looked around for Alyce as she picked up her water bucket, but there was no sign of her in the sea of faces before her.

The work began just where it had stopped the previous day. The men went back to the deep pits that they were digging in the earth, shoveling up dirt and rocks that the women carted away for the children to sift through. Peter, Julia, and Louisa moved among the

workers with their buckets, lifting dippers of water to parched and weary lips. And with each drink they gave they repeated their call to turn back to the Lord of Hosts.

They hadn't been there an hour when the earth began to shake again. It lasted only a moment, but all the workers and guards were knocked to their knees. Peter saw, far away from where they were working, that another fissure had opened up, and he could have sworn that he heard a distant scream as the rotten gasses poured out. He got to his feet and made his way to where Julia was working.

"Alyce was right," he told her through gritted teeth. "There's something evil in the earth. These earthquakes are getting closer together the farther down those men dig." He nodded toward the mine. "It's as if they're releasing something from deep down — something really horrible."

"That dark power," said Julia simply. "What could it be, do you think?"

"I've no idea. Maybe it's just a sign that the volcano is about to erupt again, or maybe … maybe it's something worse."

"Maybe it's both," said Julia contemplatively. She and Peter both turned to gaze at the peak of the volcano. Hot, acrid steam was pouring from its mouth.

"Either way, we're running out of time," said her brother.

It was just then that Peter felt a hand grip his arm. He was swung around to face a burly, foul-smelling guard. The guard leered at him, and through the haze of putrid breath Peter could see that half his teeth had rotted out of his mouth.

"Caught ourselves a thief, we have! Eh! Bruno! Look what we've got here!"

Another guard turned and came toward them. He grabbed Peter's chin and lifted up his face, peering at him through squinted eyes. "That's him all right," he grunted. "He's the one. I'd know that stinkin' face anywhere."

And then, with an ugly laugh, they each took hold of an arm and marched Peter away.

CHAPTER

13

Julia stared after them in horror, her eyes wide as saucers. She gave a choking, gasping sob and took a step forward, but then stopped herself. She could do nothing for Peter now—not just one girl against two guards. She cast her eyes frantically around for Louisa, and, seeing her close to the edge of the pit the men were digging, dropped her bucket and dipper to the ground with a splash and sprinted over to her.

Tears stung her eyes as she ran, and by the time she reached Louisa her face was a red and slimy mess of tears. She grabbed her arm and clung to her. "Peter!" she gasped. "They've taken Peter!"

"What? How?" Even with the heat of the place Louisa's face had gone absolutely white.

"The guards—they found him. They knew he was the one who had taken the map and they marched him away somewhere. I don't know what's happening to him—we have to find a way to rescue him!"

"How could we rescue him? It's just us now—and we don't have any swords or anyone on our side. We don't even know where they've taken him."

"But the people—the people we've been talking to—surely they'll help us! We'll find Alyce and she'll know what to do ..."

Louisa's ashen face looked, all of a sudden, very tired indeed. She shook her head. "They're under the threat of death as it is. We have to find a way to overthrow all the guards, not just the ones who took Peter. We can't help him until then."

Julia wanted very much to slap her. "What do we do now, then? Keep giving out water while Peter's taken captive?"

"Yes," said Louisa. "That's what the Lord of Hosts brought you here to do, isn't it?"

Louisa closed her eyes and seemed to sway back and forth. Julia began to wonder if her stepsister was ill. She watched her for a moment, mulling over what she'd said.

"Yes," Julia replied at last. "I suppose that is why we're here."

"Good," said Louisa. She opened her eyes and re-garded her stepsister. "Go get your bucket and let's get to work."

It was a long and difficult morning, punctuated by a few small tremors in the earth. None of them were large enough to do much more than slosh around the water in Julia and Louisa's buckets, but Julia was wary, remembering what Peter had said about running out of time. And so she spoke ever more urgently to the people, reminding them of all the Lord of Hosts had done for them and urging them to return to him. No one responded with much more than a nod or a grunt, or sometimes a raised eyebrow. No one seemed to rec-ognize the Deliverer of Aedyn.

As Julia moved through the crowd of prisoners she kept a close eye on her stepsister. The color hadn't returned to Louisa's face, and her eyes seemed larger and more distant with each passing hour. As she moved between the miners Julia could hear Louisa humming snippets of the song. She swayed back and forth as she sang, not quite steady on her feet. As the sun rose in the sky she seemed to wilt, her shoulders sagging in on themselves, her hand shaking each time she lifted the dipper of water to the lips of a slave. And as she faded, the singing grew louder.

Julia was desperate to keep her quiet—desperate to keep the guards from hearing the words she sang. *I must get closer to her,* she thought. *Close enough to silence her.* She wove her way nearer to her stepsister, pausing to lift the dipper of water to the lips of slaves she passed, keeping her eyes always on Louisa and praying that no one else would hear the song.

But in this she was not so fortunate.

The sun was just reaching its highest point in the sky when a guard passing nearby happened to hear Louisa's song, and stopped to listen. Julia didn't notice him until he called out.

"You there!" he cried. "That song. What's that you're singing?"

What color there had been in Louisa's face abruptly left it, and Julia thought she might be about to faint again. Julia put down the bucket of water and started toward her.

"It's … it's just an old lullaby my mother used to sing to me," Louisa was stammering. The guard gave a mirthless laugh.

"This mother of yours—she a prophetess, was she?" Louisa shook her head blankly. The guard nodded at the bucket she had in her hand. "Leave that be," he said. "We're going to pay a visit to Captain Ceres."

At this Julia rushed forward and flung an arm around Louisa's shoulders. "Let me come too," she pleaded. "She's my sister, and she's not been well … let me come too."

The guard gave a harsh nod. "Follow me."

So back up the path they went, up to the Captain's tent. Louisa walked slowly, humming all the while. Julia kept a hand on her back, urging her forward and wondering how to tell her to be quiet. They went up the ridge and were ushered into the tent.

Julia blinked rapidly, her eyes adjusting to the dim light inside. Gradually the Captain came into focus. He was sitting behind the same desk, his arms folded across his belly, listening to a guard speaking in hushed tones. Julia could only catch the odd word here and there, but it was enough for her to realize that they were talking about Louisa. "Girl ... prophecy ... singing ..." As Julia listened, hoping for some clue as to what the guards intended to do with them, her eyes were drawn once again to the Captain's talisman—why was it so familiar? Where had she seen it before?

The guard who had brought them up from the mine interrupted the other, whispering a few words in the Captain's ear. Ceres' eyebrows went up as he listened, and, as the guard finished, he leaned forward in his chair, seeming to regard Louisa as a wolf regards a lamb.

"My man tells me you've been singing a song," he said. "A song of great interest to me. Won't you sing it again for us?"

Louisa shook her head, her lips pressed tight together. Beads of sweat were starting to form on her forehead, even in the cool shade of the tent.

"Please, sir," Julia began. "My sister is sick. Out in the hot sun all day … I fear she's become delirious. She doesn't know what she's saying."

"Quiet," ordered the Captain tersely. "Let the girl speak for herself."

Julia fell quiet, silently praying as she wrung her hands. There was a moment's pause, and then Louisa opened her mouth and sang in a high, clear voice:

The two come together, the two become one,
With union comes power; control over all.

She stopped, her voice quavering on the high note, and Julia breathed an inaudible sigh of relief. But the guard who had brought them to the tent was shaking his head.

"There was more to it," he said with a scowl. "Something about light and a host returning." The Captain's eyes opened even wider.

"More to the prophecy? It cannot be. *It cannot be!*" He pushed back the chair from his desk and fairly leapt across the room, stopping when his nose was just an inch from Louisa's. "Tell me what you know, girl! Tell me quick or your life will be forfeit!" Flecks of spittle flew from his mouth to land on her face. And then, abruptly and without warning, Louisa fainted.

The Captain said a very bad word indeed and turned to Julia.

"What was it she was singing? If it was a childhood lullaby you must know it too."

"I never heard her sing it until a few days ago," Julia said truthfully. "And it was never anything but those two lines—perhaps your guard is mistaken." She paused, looking at Louisa's limp body lying at her feet. "Please, sir, let me take my sister back to our tent. She's ill—she doesn't know what she's saying."

The Captain, perhaps understanding that Louisa was useless, gave a curt nod of dismissal. "Leave me," he said. "Console your sister. My guards will bring you back to me once your sister is well."

Julia knelt and touched Louisa's face, giving it a few gentle slaps to rouse her. It was only a moment before Louisa's eyes opened, and Julia smiled for perhaps the first time that day.

"Come on," she said. "We're going back to our tent." She reached out a hand to help her stand up, then looped an arm around her back to support her. She cast one last glance at the Captain and his strange talisman, and then, just as they walked out the door, followed by one of the Captain's guards, she remembered.

The star pendant her grandmother had given her for Christmas. It was the same—it would fit right into the space in the Captain's talisman. That was the piece

they were looking for. She thought about the prophecy—
when the two halves were put together they would have
power. They would have control. But light would come,
and the Host would return ...

Julia mulled it over in her mind as they walked
back to the prisoners' tents, accompanied by the guard.
The Khemians would never find the pendant, lying
where it was on top of the dresser in her own bedroom
back in England. But they would never stop looking—
not so long as they thought it would bring them "control
over all." And as they searched the hour grew nearer
that the volcano would erupt, and some force—some
dark power—would be released into the world.

And if she could unite the talisman and the pendant, maybe she would be able to stop it. "The darkness
shall fall," she whispered to herself.

They reached the prisoners' tents, and Julia found
an empty shelter in which Louisa could rest. The guard,
silent as ever, stationed himself just outside. Julia laid
Louisa down on a cot and put a hand on her forehead.
"Sleep," she told her. "Sleep, and then we'll figure out
what to do."

Louisa nodded and closed her eyes, and Julia,
suddenly overwhelmed, wrapped her arms around her
knees, put down her head, and wept. It had all gone
wrong—Peter imprisoned, Louisa delirious, and a volcano about to erupt. She was just one girl, and she could

never save them all. She could never bring them back to the Lord of Hosts. Their prayer this morning hadn't worked, and they were all doomed.

Julia could never say how long she wept, but after a time her tears slowed and she sat back against the cot. It was time to make a plan, because crying didn't solve any problems. That was what her grandmother had always said, after all.

Grandmother. Her Christmas present. The pendant, lying back home on top of the dresser.

Her thoughts whirled faster than she could keep up with them. The pendant was back home, but if only it were here, and if she could only get the pendant that the Captain wore around his neck, the pendant into which her star would fit like a puzzle piece, she might—she *might*—be able to control whatever was about to come out of the earth. Or else she could use it as a bargaining piece for Peter's freedom—and maybe his life. The six-pointed star was the only thing she had that the Khemians wanted, and more than anything, Julia wanted her brother back.

She was confused, she was tired, and she was utterly overwhelmed. It was time to get help, she decided. It was time to find Alyce.

CHAPTER

14

High above the prisoners' tents, balancing on the uppermost branches of one of the tallest trees, a tiny bluebird, the only splash of color in an otherwise barren landscape, trilled for its mate. Louisa opened her eyes at the sound, looking around for the bird and surprised to find that she was not in her bed at home.

She opened her mouth to cry out, but all at once Julia's hand was over her mouth. "Quiet," her stepsister hissed. "We have to find Alyce, and we have to do it without that guard."

But the guard had already poked his head into the shelter. Satisfied that his prisoners were awake, he motioned for them to rise. "Come on," he said. "Captain Ceres wants to hear the rest of that song."

Julia and Louisa followed him back along the ridge to the Captain's tent. Julia kept her hand tight around Louisa's shoulders, even though Louisa seemed steadier after her long rest. The dark was falling once more, and the girls and their guard had to walk against a steady stream of prisoners returning from the mine. Julia scanned the faces of the slaves as they passed, hunting for the one woman who might know what to do. Every face looked much the same: beaten and dirty, and desperate for the help that they did not expect to come. It was impossible to distinguish one wretched face from another, so Julia could not quite believe it when a pair of gentle gray eyes leapt out at her.

"Alyce," she gasped. "Alyce!" She sprang forward, clutching the older woman's arm. The guard leapt after her. She had only a moment.

"They've taken Peter," Julia said quickly. "I don't know where he's being held. But I have what you're digging for …" The guard's meaty hand clamped tight around Julia's arm, and he dragged her away from Alyce.

"Thought you'd have a bit of a chat, did you?" he snarled, and struck her across the cheek with the back of his hand. The force of it knocked Julia to the ground, and she put up a hand to cover her face. "Get up," the guard growled again. "The Captain doesn't like to be kept waiting."

Julia struggled to her feet, casting a quick glance at Louisa. Her stepsister was standing frozen, looking blankly at the red welt that was already springing to Julia's cheek. Louisa put out a hand and touched her fingertips lightly to Julia's face, and then took her hand and squeezed it tight. "Come on," she said, and on they walked.

It was a matter of moments before they reached Ceres' tent and were ushered inside. The Captain and his guards were waiting there, standing over a figure that had collapsed on the ground.

It took Julia and Louisa a moment to recognize Peter. His face was beaten and bruised almost beyond recognition, and his bright hair was matted with something sticky and dark. Blood, Julia realized. His swollen hands had been scraped raw, and the shirt on his back lay ripped open, revealing an intricate network of bloody stripes.

He was conscious, but only barely. He looked up at his sisters and let out a groan, unable even to speak. Julia wanted to vomit, she wanted to put her hands around the captain's throat and make him suffer as Peter had suffered, she wanted to take her brother home and forget about Aedyn and Khemia and the prisoners. She trembled with the agony of it.

Louisa dropped to her knees and reached out a hand, touching the welts on Peter's shoulder. He flinched as she touched him, but then let out a breath and seemed to relax under the heat of her fingers.

"Now, perhaps the little prophetess will sing us a song," said the captain.

Louisa looked up, glancing from the Captain to Julia. She was silent.

"Sing," said the Captain after a long moment. "Sing, or I'll have my man teach you the same lesson he taught this boy here." The guard standing at Ceres' side tightened his hand around the whip at his side, and Julia gulped. But still Louisa was silent.

The guard unfurled his whip, curling his fingers around its leather handle, and then Julia stepped forward. In a high, clear voice she sang:

> The two come together, the two become one,
> With union comes power, control over all.
> Flooded by light, the shadow outdone,
> The Host shall return; the darkness shall fall.

It was a long moment before anyone spoke.

Julia's eyes were shut tight against the pain she knew must come—the sting of a whip, the crack of a hand—but none came. She opened her eyes, focusing on her brother. Peter had still not stirred, but he was casting Julia a look that she could not quite read.

"Please," she said. "My brother. Let me help my brother."

"Tell me what it means," said the Captain. His fingers were holding tight to the pendant around his neck. "Your song. 'The Host shall return.' Tell me about this host."

"It's the Lord of Hosts," said Julia. "We're his people, and this is his land—all of it. And he's going to come back. He's going to come back and then all his people will be free, and they'll never be slaves again."

She would have gone on, but the guard raised his whip and she fell silent. "Careful, girl," snarled the guard. "Careful what you say here."

The Captain cleared his throat. "This lord, girl," he said. "He'll stop a shadow?"

"I don't know what it means," said Julia, a touch of desperation coming into her voice. "All I know is that you won't be able to control whatever it is that's coming out of the earth. There's something underneath us that wants to get out—you've all felt it as well as I have. You think that if you find the second half of the pendant you'll be able to control it. You think you'll be able to take over the world. But that shadow will destroy you and anything that stands in its path. Only the Lord of Hosts can stop it."

And suddenly the Captain was on his feet, swaying a little as he stared at the girl in front of him. "How do you know about the pendant?" he demanded. "You're a slave—nothing but a slave. Tell me how you know!"

Julia remembered the weight of the six-pointed star hanging from her neck. She stood straight and still, thinking that perhaps it had been a mistake—and a bad one—to mention the pendant.

"Tell me!"

The Captain was in front of her now, his face just inches from hers, his hot, rotten breath crawling over her skin. Julia shook her head, hoping he wouldn't notice how she trembled.

"I ... I overheard a guard," she whispered. But Julia had never been a good liar and the Captain seemed to know it, for all of a sudden she realized that she was lying on the ground next to Peter. She tasted the blood in her mouth and she heard Louisa screaming, and then everything was black.

It was still dark when she awoke. Something soft pressed against her cheek, and Julia touched it gently with her fingers.

"Shh, no," said a voice that Julia hardly recognized. "The guard struck you with his whip. Leave it be for now. Try not to touch it."

"Louisa?"

"Yes. Quiet now."

"Where's Peter?"

"I think he's close. I don't know where. We're going to find him, Julia. Understand? We'll find him." Julia nodded, although it was too dark for Louisa to see her. Louisa put a cool hand to Julia's forehead, and Julia breathed a little easier at her touch. "Where are we?" she asked.

"We're in a cave close by the mine. There are guards at the entrance—I don't know how many—and …" She fell suddenly silent. "Do you hear that?"

Julia strained her ears to listen, and indeed she could make out voices, far back in the darkness. Louisa clutched her hand a little tighter as the voices fell silent, and footsteps took their place.

The two girls listened to the footsteps, coming closer and closer, step by awful step. Neither girl spoke a word, knowing that there was no place to run, no way to escape. And then…

"Julia?" said a voice that both of them knew.

CHAPTER

15

"Alyce!"

Julia stumbled into her arms, almost missing her in the darkness. "Alyce! How did you find us? Have you heard news of Peter? How did you get them to let you in?"

She was interrupted by Alyce's laughter. "Quiet, child, quiet! Enough time for all your questions. Here, I've brought you a meal." She produced a bag heavy with two loaves of bread. "Not much, I'm afraid, but it's all that the guards would allow. And I've brought someone to meet you." Even in the blackness of the cave Julia could hear the smile in her voice. "My son, Alexander. I've been telling him tales about you since before he can remember."

Julia reached out and touched the boy's shoulder, and a small, shy voice asked "Is this Lady Julia?"

"It is," she responded. "The Lord of Hosts called us once again … but I'm afraid we're not doing so well as last time."

"That is not for you to decide," said Alyce. "In the midst of the darkness you cannot understand how the Lord of Hosts is using you. Sit down and eat while I tell you a tale."

Louisa took the loaf of bread Alyce held out and tore off a chunk from the end, passing it to Julia. The girls sat back against the wall of the cave, feeling the dampness seeping beneath their clothes. They munched gratefully on the bread. It had been a long time—too long—since they had last eaten, and neither knew when they might eat again.

"Your work here has not been in vain," Alyce began. "When you gave the people water, they heard your message. There have been murmurs, rumors. The people of Aedyn know you have returned. And they will not long suffer their Deliverers to be locked up in a cave."

"Do you mean … will they …" stammered Julia, not daring to hope.

"Your presence has brought the people hope," Alyce said simply. "They are, at this moment, meeting secretly to plan your rescue. It will not be much longer, children." She glanced over her shoulder, back toward the entrance of the cave and the guards who stood watch there. "We must not tarry overlong. The attack will come before daybreak. Be ready when it comes. You and your brother"—Alyce dropped her voice—"You have a plan, of course. A plan to take us all back to Aedyn. The Lord of Hosts told you what to do, just like last time." She spoke with a quiet certainty, and Julia had not the heart to tell her that the Lord of Hosts had been silent. She had no idea how to get the prisoners back to Aedyn— no idea where the boats were kept and no idea how to sail them if she did.

"Of course," Julia said quickly. "Of course we have a plan." And even in the darkness she could sense Alyce's smile.

"I thank the Lord of Hosts that you've returned," she said. "And I thank him that my son has seen this day, and that he will have such a tale to tell his children."

"They said I can't fight," Alexander put in. "They said I'm too small, and I'll just get in the way."

"There will be time enough to fight," said his mother gently. "Time enough, when your height matches the size of your courage." She pulled both of the girls into a quick embrace. "By daybreak. Be ready."

"We'll be ready," promised Julia, in as confident a voice as she could muster. Alyce took her son's hand and led him out toward the entrance of the cave.

"You have a plan?" Louisa asked as soon as they were gone.

Julia was quiet for a very, very long moment.

"I'm sure we'll think of something," she said finally.

Through the entrance to the cave Julia and Louisa watched as the small patch of sky turned from gray to dusky purple to black. There were no stars they could see—none that were not covered by the gloomy smoke that spewed from the volcano and blanketed the island in clouds.

"So this plan," said Louisa.

"Stop it," Julia snapped. "You know I haven't got a plan."

"Then maybe you should think of something?" suggested Louisa. "While we're waiting, I mean."

Julia nodded, then leaned back against the wall of the cave and closed her eyes. "The first thing is to get the Captain's talisman," she said.

"Why?"

"Because it's the second half," said Julia. "Do you remember the pendant my grandmother sent me for Christmas?"

"It was something odd, wasn't it? Shaped like a star?"

"Yes. Made of a green sort of stone, with six points. And it would fit just exactly into that talisman the Captain wears around his neck."

"And what will happen if you put the two halves together?" Louisa asked.

Julia gave her stepsister a look. "What did you think your song was about?"

Louisa sat back and thought very hard. *"The shadow outdone, the Host shall return,"* she remembered. "So if you get your pendant from home, and put it together with the Captain's ..."

"Exactly," said Julia.

"Well, that makes things much simpler," said Louisa. "How, exactly, are you going to get your pendant?"

"That's the part I'm still working on."

"Ah." And the girls were silent again.

Neither knew quite how long the silence lasted before they heard a new sound outside, coming from the mouth of the cave. Footsteps. Shouts. A cry—of triumph or of pain they could not tell.

"How many do you think there are?" breathed Louisa into Julia's ear. "How many have come to rescue us?"

"I've no idea. If only it wasn't so dark ..." Julia shook her head. "Come on. Let's get closer to the entrance. Maybe we can slip out." She stood and put out a hand to help Louisa to her feet.

The two girls made their way to the entrance of the cave. The only light came from a torch the guards had stuck into the ground a few steps away, but even its meager glow seemed bright after the darkness of the cave. Julia could make out a few figures—two wearing Khemian armor, the others dressed in the rags of the prisoners. The prisoners seemed armed with little more than rocks and sticks, but they were fighting with all the strength and courage of men of Aedyn.

Julia knew exactly what to do. She and Louisa were going to make their way out of the cave without being noticed—it would be easy, in this gloom—and they would get behind the prisoners. Then she would call out and announce that she was free, and that she had been sent to deliver the prisoners. They would rally to her, and the guards would be overwhelmed. The Captain would hand over his talisman without any fuss. It would be easy.

She turned to Louisa and whispered, "Follow me." She reached out and took her stepsister's hand, and they crept along the wall toward the entrance of the cave. And then they stopped cold in their tracks, for they could see another figure by the pale light of the torch. Something that was not a man …

Julia froze.

The Gul'nog swung his massive arms through the band of prisoners, scattering them right and left like so many matchsticks. Even the Khemian guards cowered before it. No one was foolish enough to fight it—they simply fled, and Julia felt the hope sinking within her.

The single torch had been knocked over in the confusion—perhaps by one of the guards, perhaps by the Gul'nog. Julia watched as the dim glow became brighter, the fire spreading slowly at first, then more swiftly. The girls could feel the wave of heat on their faces and arms—a heat entirely different than the dense, muggy air to which they had become accustomed.

The fire illuminated the land around the cave, every blade of grass casting a long, sharp shadow over its neighbor. Each rock, each tree stood out starkly, and by the light of the fire Julia watched as the prisoners fled. And then the fire engulfed the mouth of the cave, and they could see nothing but the flames in front of them.

Neither Julia nor Louisa had ever experienced heat like this before. Julia had burned her hand once on a hot pan—not badly—just enough for her to remember the sting. But this heat was new. The searing air singed their faces, and both girls shrank back into the cooler depths of the cave. The rock floor was damp—there was nothing to burn in the cave, and they would be safe until the fire and the Gul'nog had both passed them by.

They retreated further and further back, away from the crackling heat and the choking smoke that filled their lungs. Julia had never thought that a fire could be so loud—had never thought that it could boom in her ears

until all other sounds were drowned out. And so it was
that she barely heard the roar of the Gul'nog, and when
she turned around she saw a monster in flames.

He had come through the fire for them. This
creature of night and shadow—he had sensed the presence of the Deliverer, and he had leapt through a blaze
that would kill a man. Flames licked his face, his arms,
his legs, but he seemed unharmed. He opened wide his
mouth and roared again.

Louisa's fingers slackened in Julia's hand, and
without a word she slumped to the ground. Julia fell to
her hands and knees, feeling Louisa's limp body beside
her. There was nothing to do. Nothing to do but wait for
the Gul'nog, and whatever horrors he had in mind for
the Deliverer. There was no place to run, nowhere they
could go to escape. And so Julia closed her eyes and, in
her last moments, breathed up a prayer. It was a prayer
without words, without hope, without expectation.

But it was enough.

With a rush of wind another figure came through
the flames. Julia opened her eyes and at first could hardly
make out what it was—a creature that seemed not to
touch the earth, that tore at the Gul'nog with claws and
wings and ...

Wings. It was the falcon—the falcon that had
brought them across the sea! Julia stifled a cry as she real-

ized who had come. She wanted to go forward—wanted to throw her arms around the falcon—but she held back, watching the two dark figures battle against the glare of the fire. The falcon's claws were deadly, tearing at the Gul'nog's flesh and doing the damage that the fire could not.

The Gul'nog fought back, his fists tearing into the falcon's wings, trying to cripple it and end the attack. But the falcon was the monster's equal in strength and size, and the battle seemed to go on and on, neither side gaining any ground. Julia watched, hardly daring to move, hardly daring to breathe, certain that any second might be the falcon's last.

And then, in the space of an instant, it happened. The falcon's claw slashed through the air, and one of its talons sliced into the Gul'nog's eye. The monster gave an unearthly cry and crumpled to the ground, both fists clutched tight to his face. And Julia was screaming, screaming with all the air left in her lungs, screaming even as the falcon turned and fixed its great eye upon her.

All the breath left her lungs as she looked into that eye. It seemed to hold all the pain of the world, all the wisdom of the ages. The falcon came toward her, slowly—it was tired, Julia realized. By the light of the fire that still raged outside she could see that its feathers were singed around the edges, and there were tiny rivulets of dark blood trickling down its chest.

It bent its head, its eye on a level with hers, and Julia instantly understood that she was meant to climb on its back.

"But where?" she asked. "Where will you take me?"

The falcon didn't answer, but jerked its head to the side in that curious way of birds. Julia understood. *Home.*

"No," said Julia. "Peter's been taken away and Louisa's fainted over there. I know the pendant's back at home, I know that without the pendant the volcano will explode and we won't be able to stop that dark power, but I *can't* leave Peter and Louisa here. I *won't.*"

And then something happened that Julia did not expect. The falcon tilted its head again, opened its beak, and let out a shrill cry. And then, out of the shadows, stepped an old man swathed in the dark robes of a monk. A man Julia knew well.

With a little cry Julia ran forward into his arms. It was Giaus — Giaus who had saved their lives in Aedyn more times than she could remember. The monk held her in a tight embrace, then lifted up her chin and looked deep into her eyes.

"The volcano is going to explode with or without the pendant," he said, in a voice as warm and rich as she'd remembered. "The mine has gotten too deep, and the tremors are getting worse. You've seen this for yourself. The Khemians know that the power in the earth will finally be released. They think that with the united talisman they'll be able to control it, but we both know," he said, "that there is only one force in all the worlds that can control a dark power such as this."

"The Lord of Hosts," said Julia.

"He can destroy these demons," said Gaius, "but if the power is unchecked it will take over our whole world. The two parts of the talisman must be united before the light can return."

"I don't understand," Julia insisted. "Why does the Lord of Hosts depend on a talisman to come back to his people?"

"The Lord of Hosts never left," replied the monk. "But he has given us clues and tools to find his presence. We don't know what will happen when the two halves come together, but the prophecy tells us we will be flooded with light." Giaus moved closer, and his arm came around Julia in an embrace. "We can't know everything all at once, dear one. There's always a mystery while we wait for the story to unfold."

Julia nodded, considering this. "So I have to go home," she said. "I have to go home to get the star pendant. And I have to go quickly, because"—she turned over her shoulder to look at the still form of her stepsister, lying in the shadows of the cave—"because there might not be much time left."

"There is never enough time for all the good we wish to do in the world," the falcon said. "But there is no time to hesitate."

"What about Peter? I don't know where he's being kept—I can't go home without him. What if he's hurt? What if he needs me? And Louisa—do we leave her here?"

"Your brother and sister are under the protection of the Lord of Hosts," said the falcon. A stern note had come into his voice. "It is time for you to do what is necessary, my child. You must find the pendant and bring it back here."

He bent his knees and ducked his head in a sort of bow. Julia put out her hand to touch the top of its head, stroking the feathers at the crest of its head with a gentle hand. She hoisted herself up onto the falcon's back, steadying herself between its wings and putting her arms tight around its neck.

"We must go through the fire," the falcon told her. "Don't be afraid. Hold tight." And then he gave a strong beat of his mighty wings and rose up into the sky. Julia clung tight to its neck as the air whistled around her, and then she was soaring, soaring, up over the edge of the world.

CHAPTER
16

Peter, lying in the darkness, woke to find that he could hardly move. His hands and feet had been tied with thick, coarse ropes, and his whole body felt bruised and broken. He shrugged his shoulders, trying to twist himself into an upright position. The movement brought a gasp of pain to his lips. He had been beaten, and badly, then shoved in this cave like a common criminal. Which, Peter realized, he was.

He groaned as he sat up. He tugged experimentally at the ropes that bound him, realizing quickly that it was useless. He could never untie those knots, especially not with his fingers so swollen and bruised.

It was quiet outside. No moon, no wind — just that horrid smell from the volcano, and the dank air that stifled every breath. And then, as he listened, there came a sound. Twigs breaking. Grasses rustling. Footsteps — slow and soft, but sure. Peter leaned forward, trying to make out the figure that was coming toward the cave. His eyes had adjusted to the dark of the cave, but there was no light from anywhere, and no way to see who it was. Peter breathed in deeply, willing himself to be still, willing his heart to stop crashing against his chest. He thought that whoever was coming must be able to find him by the beating of his heart ...

The footsteps stopped when they were just inside the cave. There was a long moment of silence, and then:

"Peter?" said a voice.

A guard wouldn't have stopped to ask his name. It must be another one of the prisoners, thought Peter. It must be a friend. "Yes!" he called out. "Yes, it's me. I'm here. They've tied me up."

A man came forward, moving toward the sound of Peter's voice. He knelt down beside him, feeling for the ropes that bound his arms and legs. Finding them, he withdrew a knife and began to saw at the bonds.

"My name is Gregory," he said as he cut. "I am a friend of Alyce. She told me that the Deliverers had returned, and then I heard your message at the mine. I and my brothers will fight for you, and will follow where you lead."

"Wonderful," muttered Peter, grimacing as Gregory's knife strained against the ropes. He thought that perhaps this would not be the ideal time to inform Gregory that he had no plan, no mission ... just a vague idea that he needed to get the Captain's talisman away from him.

The knife broke through the ropes binding his hands, and Peter rubbed his wrists as Gregory moved to his feet. The skin was raw and broken where the cords had cut into his skin. "We have to get to the Captain," he told Gregory. "The Captain wears ..."

But then he stopped, for there were more footsteps outside. Different steps. And not those of a friend. Gregory froze, and even in the dim light of the cave Peter could see that he was trembling.

"It's the Gul'nog," said Gregory. He returned to the ropes binding Peter's ankles, sawing fiercely. One by one the ropes broke away, and finally Peter was free. He scrambled to his feet, trying to make as little noise as possible.

"Should we ..."

"Quiet," said Gregory in a whisper. "Quiet. He must be looking for us—or the others who are coming."

"Others?"

"Hush."

They waited together in the gloom of the cave, and as they waited they heard a scuffle, and shouts, and finally they could see that one of the guards' torches had been knocked to the ground, and the flame was spreading like a wildfire.

Peter and Gregory crept to the mouth of the cave and looked out. Against the backdrop of the flames they could see the Gul'nog, and a few dark figures who had been unlucky enough to stand in its way. And then, as they watched, the Gul'nog leapt through the flames and was gone.

"Run," said Gregory. *"Run!"*

Peter needed no urging. Mindless of the ache in his legs he urged them forward, out of the cave and into the forest that lay beyond. He could feel the heat of the fire between his shoulders, and he remembered running like this in Aedyn, running away from a cannon that was about to explode, running for his life without any certainty that he would be spared.

He ran deep into the trees. His lungs were on fire, and finally he collapsed against a massive oak, breathing hard and praying that he hadn't been seen. He'd left behind the heat of the fire, but he could still hear the roaring and crackling of the flames. Had he been followed?

Gregory had spoken of others—had the prisoners rebelled? Had Julia and Louisa been set free? So many unknowns ... and the only certainty was that he had to get the Captain's talisman.

It wouldn't be dark much longer, thought Peter, looking up at the sky. The slaves would be back at the mine soon. Maybe the Captain was still asleep, and Peter could steal the talisman from around his neck. A slim chance ... but he had to try.

Peter got to his feet, looked around, and promptly realized that he was lost. He didn't know these woods, and had no idea where the mine was. If he could just find the volcano ...

The trees were thick, and blocked any view he might have had. He needed to find a ridge—needed to get higher up so he could see. Or else he could go back the way he'd come. Surely there would be a road ... but he promptly abandoned that idea. There was also fire, and the Gul'nog. He'd have to find his way through the woods.

Peter fished his father's compass out of his pocket and flicked open the top, watching as the needle spun around. He closed his eyes and tried to remember the map that he and Julia had studied only the previous night. The woods, the volcano, the caves ... he couldn't remember which direction he should go, and had no idea how far it would be.

South, he decided abruptly. He'd go south, and see what he found along the way.

The going was hard. Every muscle ached, and wounds that had not yet healed were screaming for rest. But still Peter pressed on. For all he knew Julia and Louisa were being held captive somewhere, having worse wounds inflicted on them. The only way to stop all this was to get the talisman.

He'd been right about the night ending soon. Dawn was pressing against the sky, illuminating a broken, barren landscape. The stagnant air pressed in on him. The smell of sulfur seemed to grow worse as he walked—perhaps he was, after all, getting closer to the volcano. He tripped over rocks and ducked under low-hanging branches, almost weeping once when he stumbled and gashed open his knee. The blood was bright—the only color in a gray landscape. Peter ripped off a strip of fabric from his shirt and blotted up the blood, then straightened his leg and kept walking. Whoever those "others" were that Gregory had spoken of, one thing was certain: they would never come to rescue him here.

And then he was there.

The trees opened up on a familiar scene—the mine, crawling with soldiers and prisoners. The guards, Peter noticed, seemed crueler than before. They kept their whips curled in their hands, not at their sides, and used them freely on any prisoner who was falling behind. Peter scanned the area for his sisters, but didn't see Julia's bright hair or Louisa's familiar shape in the crowd. He was alone.

But another figure did come into view—a figure Peter knew well. The Captain. He was moving among the prisoners, using his whip with a steady hand, and even at this distance Peter could hear the curses coming from his mouth.

Smoke and ash were pouring from the mouth of the volcano, and the ground beneath Peter's feet seemed to tremble almost constantly. The eruption was coming—and soon. There wasn't much time left—even the Captain could tell that, evidently. But how to get the talisman?

Peter watched the Captain, remembering his fights with Mason back at school. He'd bested larger boys before, but a trained soldier? It would be like attacking his father, Peter thought.

He threw off the thought. It was something a child would think, and he was a man now. And so he kept his eye on the Captain, watching how he moved, looking for a weakness. But the man moved like the old solider he was: practiced, steady, with muscles taut and ready. There would be no opening—no opportunity to take the talisman without the Captain's fist connecting with Peter's windpipe.

Peter started forward anyway, making his way into the crowd of prisoners. He was closer to the Captain now—close enough to see the talisman swinging from a thin leather cord around his neck.

The volcano belched more smoke and ash, and Peter felt the ground give way underneath him. The earth seemed to tilt this way and that; all around him prisoners and guards alike were screaming as they fell and clutched at the ground. It was an earthquake stronger than any he had ever felt, and Peter knew what it meant.

But amid the screams Peter looked up and saw that the Captain, too, had collapsed on the ground and was struggling to regain his balance. And suddenly it was easy.

With the fleetness of foot that belongs only to the young, Peter dashed forward and knelt beside the aging soldier. He thrust a firm hand under the Captain's chin, grasped the talisman, and, with a swift jerk, tore away the leather cord.

He was ten steps away before the Captain could yell, and fifteen before Peter could hear the guards stumbling to pursue him. They never had a chance. Running, running harder and faster than he ever had before, Peter was in the woods, the talisman held tight in his hot fist. He'd forgotten his aching shoulders, forgotten the sting of the reopened wound on his knee. He was running, and the soldiers could never keep up.

He kept running long after he knew that the guards had lost him. He ran deeper and deeper into the woods, hardly thinking of what lay behind. He splashed into a trickle of a stream, then up the opposite bank ... and then he stopped short, because he could hardly believe what he saw in front of him.

CHAPTER

17

By the slant of the sun shining through the window, Julia could see that it was late afternoon. Supper soon, she thought, and then snuggled deeper under the covers. Bed was so lovely, so warm, even at this time of the day. She closed her eyes and breathed deeply, ready to fall back asleep.

No. Supper. She would be expected to be dressed. With a frustrated sigh Julia extricated herself from the mess of blankets and padded over to the dresser. She could feel the December chill in the air, even in the sun, and she rummaged through the drawers for a sweater.

And then she stopped short, because lying there on top of the dresser, beside a photograph of her mother and the copy of *Alice in Wonderland* that Peter had given her, lay a six-pointed star cut out of an odd, greenish stone.

Khemia. The pendant. The prophecy.

It all came back to her in an instant. The fire, the Gul'nog, the falcon—where had he gone? She remembered flying on its back, flying into the dawn. She remembered a flash, and then … nothing. Nothing until she woke up, warm in her bed.

Julia reached out and picked up the pendant, turning it over and over in her hand. And then, feeling mightily foolish, she called out in a hoarse whisper: "Falcon! Falcon!"

It didn't come. How would she ever get back to Khemia if it didn't come? *"Falcon!"* she said again, louder this time, and then she heard footsteps on the stairs.

The door to her room opened slowly, revealing a thin, gaunt woman with hard eyes. Her stepmother. She looked Julia over and sniffed.

"I see you're awake," she said. "Thought you'd caught your death of cold out there. I suppose you still won't tell us where your brother is?"

Julia shook her head mutely. Her stepmother heaved a mighty sigh. "Your father's still out searching. No telling if he'll find him—not with another cold night coming on. It's a miracle you survived the first." She gave Julia a hard look, and the corners of her mouth twisted up into something like a smirk. "Thought you'd be the little heroine and run away, did you? I look forward to seeing what punishment your father has devised for you. Get dressed, now. Cook will have supper ready soon." And she shut the door behind her.

Tears welled up in Julia's eyes as she stared after her stepmother. She had to get back to Khemia—had to get back *now*. She grasped the star pendant so hard that its points cut into her hand. If the falcon wouldn't come to her, well, she would have to go find it herself.

She threw on the warmest clothes she could find and stomped into her winter boots. She didn't know how long she'd have to be outside, and she could always discard the extra layers once she was back in Aedyn. She opened the bedroom door slowly, carefully, praying that it wouldn't creak, and started down the stairs. But before she descended she stopped and hurried back up to Peter's room. He kept an electric torch hidden in his dresser, stuffed underneath all his socks. She dug through the woolen mess, wondering why on *earth* he couldn't keep the drawer organized, and then her fingers closed on it.

She pulled the torch out of the drawer, slammed it shut, and snuck down the stairs and outside. It was just as cold as it had been that Christmas morning— colder, perhaps, with the sun just starting to set. She breathed out, watching her frozen breath hanging for a moment in the air.

Julia shoved the torch into one of her pockets and strode along the path to the river, just as she and Peter had done before. It felt like ages ago, she thought. So much had changed since that morning. They'd been back to Aedyn. They'd been called to save the prisoners. She'd ridden on a falcon …

Now that she was alone and in the open air there was no need to be silent. She cupped her hands around her mouth and cried out, as loud as she could. "Falcon! *Falcon!*" She searched the skies for any sign of it, hoping for the familiar sight of its broad wings swooping down for her. But the skies were empty.

Julia heaved a mighty sigh and trudged into the woods. She may as well make for the stream. If the falcon wouldn't come, she'd have to get into Aedyn another way.

It wasn't long before she reached the water. It had frozen over in the cool nights since that Christmas morning, and it was hard enough for Julia to walk on. She stomped on the ice angrily — how was she supposed to get back if that portal wouldn't open?

When a sharp stamp with her boot failed to break through the ice, Julia sat down on the bank of the river put her chin in her hands. *Think*, she told herself. *Think. There must be a way back, or the Lord of Hosts would never have sent me to get the pendant.*

The Lord of Hosts. Of course.

Julia shut her eyes tight and prayed as hard as she knew how. "Take me back," she whispered. "I want to help your people, and I know you can hear me, even in this world. Take me back to Khemia."

She opened her eyes, expecting to see the river flowing and swirling as it had been before. But nothing had changed.

Julia lifted her head to look for the falcon, but night was falling. It was too dark to see much of anything in the sky. Julia rifled in her pockets for Peter's torch, fumbling with her chilled fingers. She clicked on the switch, and a bright beam of light illuminated the opposite bank.

But something had changed. The trees—the shadows were all different. There was an odd smell that hung in the air. And the cold … the cold was gone.

Julia stood and looked around, her eyes wide. Could it be … could it possibly be …

"Julia!"

She looked up and gasped. It was Peter, looking like he'd just run a race. He was panting and sweat was dripping down his forehead, and something awful seemed to have happened to his knee.

"Peter, what …"

"I've got the talisman," Peter interrupted. He held out his hand, revealing the green stone that lay within. "I got it from the Captain. There was an earthquake, and

I took it. I think … I think the volcano …" He doubled over, choking, gasping for breath.

"Here," said Julia. "I've been home. I have the other piece." She pulled it out of her pocket.

Peter opened his mouth to ask her how she'd gotten home, how any of this had happened, when there came a roar that sounded like the end of the world. Both children looked up, above the trees, and saw that the ash spewing from the mouth of the volcano had filled the sky. The crest of the mountain collapsed in on itself, the rocks crashing and tumbling over themselves in a mighty cascade. It was the end.

And as they watched the eruption something new came out of the earth—something that was neither ash nor lava. A shadow, a wraith, and it seemed to unfold itself from the rocks and reach out towards the sky. Julia felt all the courage leach out of her as she watched the figure growing, growing, growing.

"There's no time left," said Peter. "Here." He held out the Captain's talisman, and Julia took the star in her hand and fit it into the piece that Peter held. The two halves locked together, and a thread of light shone for a moment in the space where they met.

"What happens now?" said Julia.

Peter looked at his sister and shook his head. "We wait," he said. And they both held tight to the pendant as the shadow filled the sky.

EPILOGUE

L ouisa opened her eyes, blinking as her vision adjusted to the darkness. The cave, she thought. She was still in the cave. But Julia—where had Julia gone?

She stood and crept along the cave wall, stopping when she came to the entrance. She blinked in the half-light of morning, shielding her face from the sunlight. The ground outside was charred, and as she poked at the earth with the toe of her shoe a swirl of ash rose into the wind.

She watched the ash swirling, rising, and then, as she lifted her eyes, she saw something else. It was a shadow ... a shadow that seemed to grow more substantial as it spread itself over the sky. Louisa shrank back into the cave, wondering where she could hide, wondering if Peter and Julia were safe.

And then there came a light, brighter by far than the shadow, stronger than any light Louisa had seen. It was as if the sun had come to earth. And the sound, like a thousand bells, reverberating inside her head. Louisa fell back to the ground and stared, her eyes burning. She couldn't close them, couldn't look away from the light. The light was speaking to her, calling to her.

She stood and walked out of the cave, following the path down to the mine. It was time.

Share Your Thoughts

With the Author: Your comments will be forwarded to the author when you send them to *zauthor@zondervan.com*.

With Zondervan: Submit your review of this book by writing to *zreview@zondervan.com*.

Free Online Resources at
www.zondervan.com

Zondervan AuthorTracker: Be notified whenever your favorite authors publish new books, go on tour, or post an update about what's happening in their lives at www.zondervan.com/authortracker.

Daily Bible Verses and Devotions: Enrich your life with daily Bible verses or devotions that help you start every morning focused on God. Visit www.zondervan.com/newsletters.

Free Email Publications: Sign up for newsletters on Christian living, academic resources, church ministry, fiction, children's resources, and more. Visit www.zondervan.com/newsletters.

Zondervan Bible Search: Find and compare Bible passages in a variety of translations at www.zondervanbiblesearch.com.

Other Benefits: Register yourself to receive online benefits like coupons and special offers, or to participate in research.

ZONDERVAN

ZONDERVAN.com/
AUTHORTRACKER
follow your favorite authors